Sherlock Holmes
Playing the Game

Cenarth Fox

Sherlock Holmes—Playing the Game

First published in 2020 by Fox Plays
www.cenfoxbooks.com
www.foxplays.com

ISBN 978 0 949175 42 7

Cover design by Oliviaprodesign

Playing the Game

If you are 'playing the game', you believe the following:
Sherlock Holmes was a real person.
Dr Watson, another real person, wrote the stories.
Arthur Conan Doyle, a *really* real person, was Dr Watson's literary
agent who promoted the tales, helping to get them published.

*"I used occasionally to read detective stories. It always annoyed me
how in the old-fashioned detective stories, the detective always
seemed to get at his results either by some lucky chance or fluke or
else it was quite unexplained how he got there. He got there but he
never gave an explanation how, and that didn't seem to me to be
playing the game."*
Sir Arthur Conan Doyle—1927

The Changing Calendar

Dates within this novel have been fed flexibility.

For
Kirk Alexander
The actor who played Sherlock Holmes in
The Real Sherlock Holmes
Sherlock, Stock and Barrel
and *Nursing Holmes*

Chapter 1

WHAT A MESS. Sherlock Holmes was rarely tidy, and right now his sitting-room had lost all self-respect. The great detective didn't care. He was soon to retire; off to Sussex and a new life as an apiarist. Meet beekeeper Holmes.

He and friend, Dr John H. Watson, first arrived at 221B Baker Street as relatively young men. Now, with both in their seventh decade and no longer solving mysteries, retirement with honey, at least for Holmes, beckoned.

He'd been packing for days. A massive trunk dominated the room and, scattered about higgledy-piggledy, were portmanteaus, small leather handbags, and a double leather hat box, all being filled with the detritus of his decades in London. There was even an ancient tea-chest courtesy of the Honourable East India Company, and, in hiding, Watson's travel-worn and battered tin dispatch-box stood proud within the clutter.

It was late, Holmes was exhausted and, trying to pack his precious possessions, he dropped his magnifying lens. It lay on the floor behind the settee. To retrieve the lens, Holmes stepped over piles of books and knelt. With the object in hand, he attempted to rise. 'Ow!' he yelled as his rheumatism came out to play and strong pain kept him on the floor. He fumed then called.

'Mrs. Hudson.' Silence. He bellowed. 'Mrs Hudson!'

The landlady called from outside the room. 'I'm here, Mr. Holmes.'

With difficulty, she entered carrying a tray of goodies. Older than her famous tenant and frail to boot, she looked in vain for a place to rest the refreshments. The chairs housed bags, books and beakers.

The table disappeared beneath papers, pipes and periodicals together with a violin case and numerous bits 'n bobs from cases investigated and solved over many years. Mrs. Hudson shook her head.

'Oh, Mr Holmes, you are indeed the worst tenant in London. There is nowhere to place the tray.' Seeing no-one, she hesitated. Was she alone? 'Mr Holmes?'

His face appeared above the back of the settee. 'Good evening, Mrs Hudson.'

Once, a sudden appearance by Holmes would have startled her, but no longer. Having endured years of his unusual behaviour, which included discharging a firearm many times in this very room, she simply awaited an explanation. He spoke.

'I am having difficulty in standing.'

She sighed. 'Oh, it's your rheumatism again.'

'That is an excellent deduction, madam; you have skipped *removing the impossible* and plumped for *what goes without saying.*'

His sarcasm too was ignored. 'May I be of assistance?' she asked.

'If you would be so kind,' said Holmes and dropped out of sight.

Now Mrs Hudson found herself in a quandary. She couldn't help her tenant until the tea tray found a place of rest. She continued searching.

As she did so, the detective's face appeared again. 'Is there a problem, dear lady? My pain threshold plummets by the minute.'

'You have so many things, Mr Holmes; I cannot find a spot for the tray.'

'What's wrong with the floor?'

'The floor?' she replied, aghast. 'You want me to place the tea tray on the floor?'

'Oh please, madam, place it somewhere, *any*where, but kindly give me a hand.'

Mrs Hudson could see no other solution. Carefully she bent to place the tray on what clear space remained on the rug in front of the hearth. She, more than Holmes, suffered with ageing bones, and so endured a painful process to lower a tray with cups and saucers, milk and sugar, cake on a plate, a tea-strainer and a full teapot complete with tartan cosy. She worried things might spill or break. In the end she managed to kneel and set the tray on the floor. She paused, and from behind the settee came a new serve of sarcasm.

'I'm admiring the handiwork of this furniture-maker, Mrs Hudson. Have you observed his joinery skills?'

No reply was heard as Mrs Hudson and tray were on the floor, and neither seemed capable of moving.

'Mr Holmes?'

'I'm still here, Mrs Hudson.'

'I'm afraid I can't get up.' His rheumatism proved to be contagious.

Holmes groaned. 'Oh, it's not you as well.'

'Shall I ring for help?'

His sarcasm shifted gears. 'What a splendid idea. And any time this week would suit me.'

Mrs Hudson spied the small bell on a side table. She shuffled closer and reached for it. No, she couldn't make it past the obstacles.

'Mr Holmes?'

'Is that you, Mrs Hudson?'

'I'm afraid I can't reach the bell.'

'Never mind; it'll be Christmas soon, and we can get the goose to give us a hand. Did you know Mrs Oakshott in Brixton Road has the finest birds in London?'

'With the finest jewels in their non-existent crops; or so I'm told.'

Holmes paused. *What did she say?* He felt discombobulated. Did he ever? His voice changed in pitch and volume. 'I beg your pardon?'

'Perhaps we should test Dr Watson's knowledge of anseriformes anatomy.'

What on earth is she talking about? He returned to the matter at hand. 'You were considering a career in campanology, madam.'

'Actually I've remembered. Ringing the bell won't be much help.'

'Why, is the goose deaf?'

'No, you see, I'm already here.'

Both tenant and landlady were slowing down, physically, even mentally. And now, alone, they were stuck, forcing Holmes to find another solution. He decided to bite the bullet.

Grasping the top of the settee, he sucked in a deep breath, and heaved himself skywards. As pain savaged his nervous system, his roar echoed around the room. Standing upright, he took pride in his achievement. His landlady beamed.

'Oh, well done, Mr Holmes; bravo.'

Holmes muttered. 'There must be something I can take to dull this wretched pain.'

As he escaped from behind the settee, Mrs Hudson raised a hand as if hailing a hansom cab. Holmes approached the kneeling landlady, about to demonstrate chivalry was alive and well, when he spotted something. Ignoring Mrs Hudson, he headed for the table.

'*There* it is,' he exclaimed, seizing a book and walking away from the kneeling woman.

Mrs Hudson shook her head. Nothing the detective did surprised her. She'd seen the complete range of responses from Sherlock Holmes. And so, using a chair for support, she helped herself to stand.

'No need for your assistance, Mr Holmes, but thank you for offering.'

Holmes heard nothing as he devoured his new-found book. 'This is wonderful,' he purred, then stopped. 'Did you say something?'

'Would you like tea, Mr Holmes?' He waved a dismissive hand and resumed reading. She cleared a space on the table, bent, and with considerable difficulty transported the tray to its rightful place. She poured herself a cup of tea. 'I have some Madeira cake, Mr Holmes.'

He kept reading. She moved a hat and books from a chair, sat, and sipped her tea; the only sound being the clinking of her cup and saucer. After some time, Holmes looked up in shock.

'Mrs Hudson?' he queried, the end of his question rising in pitch.

She raised her cup. 'Good evening, sir.'

'You're sitting at *my* table drinking *my* tea in *my* sitting-room.'

The landlady returned serve with her own shot of sarcasm. 'Your powers of observation are as sharp as ever, Mr Holmes.'

The detective put down his book, moved to the mantelpiece, and to the Persian slipper containing his tobacco. 'Do you have an explanation for this extraordinary behaviour?'

'I thought we should celebrate the end of our time together here in Baker Street.'

'Celebrate? Whatever for?'

'Dr Watson described you as an automaton, a calculating machine, but I believe even you might harbour a smidgeon of emotion at such a time as this.'

'You believe in vain, madam, and Watson was right. Now please feel free to leave.' He lit his pipe.

The landlady nodded. *Typical Mr Holmes*, she thought as she drained her cup, placed it and the saucer on the tray, stood and walked to the door. She opened it and paused.

'And you are definitely leaving by the end of the week?' she asked.

He sighed from boredom. 'Yes, madam; we agreed upon the date some time ago.'

'Thank you but it's just that I cannot visit the editor until you have officially retired.' She smiled and stepped out of the room. Her head appeared. 'Good night, Mr Holmes.' She left, closing the door.

It was rare for Sherlock Holmes to be lost for words, but speechless he became. The landlady's words, *I cannot visit the editor*, ignited the detective's brain. His dolichocephalic head fairly buzzed. It took a few seconds for him to respond but when he did, the landlady clearly heard her tenant's stentorian tones.

'Mrs Hudson!'

Holmes strode to the door and flung it open preparing to shout again. His landlady stood facing him with a friendly expression, and clutching to her bosom some pages tied with a ribbon. She'd placed the material in the hall beforehand. He stood back, gestured and she entered.

'Shall I remove the tray, Mr Holmes?'

'Not before you explain your intriguing remark—if you would be so kind.'

The landlady relished the moment. Rarely did she have the detective's full attention, and could not recall any occasion in which she held the upper hand in a conversation with her lodger. Most of their conversations were either trivial or perfunctory. Placing her pages on the crowded table, she sat, which in itself was most unusual.

'Mr Holmes, I made a promise to myself I would not say a word until after you have actually departed.'

The mystery deepened and with it, his frustration.

'You speak in riddles, madam. Kindly elucidate.'

She paused, milked the moment then confessed. 'I have written a book, sir, about my life as landlady to the world's greatest consulting detective and his friend and colleague.' She patted the pages.

For the second time that evening, Holmes became momentarily speechless. Even with his superior intellect and razor-sharp wit, it took time for his brain to process this latest news. His mind raced. *Mrs Hudson has written a book. Mrs Hudson is an author? Mrs Hudson has written a book about me.*

'A book?' he queried.

'It's a true account of the life and work of two great men—Dr John H. Watson and your own good self.'

'I see.' He didn't see but refused to admit his confusion.

'But I shall never show my manuscript to an editor until you have definitely retired.'

'How kind,' he said without a sliver of kindness in his voice.

'It would be quite wrong of me to have your idiosyncrasies revealed to the world while you are still solving mysteries.'

'My idiosyncrasies?' muttered Holmes. He never spluttered but this time almost broke his duck.

'I believe the editor of *The Strand Magazine* should be my first port of call. Do you know the gentleman?'

Holmes didn't, and the problem the detective now faced became which question to ask first. Every statement uttered by his landlady created another question, even questions. In the verbal duelling stakes, she led by a country mile, and before he could begin to cross-examine Mrs Hudson, she continued.

'Unquestionably your legions of followers know every detail of your outstanding sleuthing, but alas, Mr Holmes, they know little or nothing of your private life.'

Holmes put aside his good manners, and his tone matched that of an outraged person stating a phrase such as *how dare you!*

'My private life?!'

'Of course I would never reveal any of your *really* annoying habits.'

His pitch and volume increased. '*Really* annoying habits?!'

'One of which is repeating everything I say.'

The conversation stopped. For Holmes, the penny dropped. He'd been outfoxed and outboxed but now his concerns vanished. Calm returned. A trace of a smile tip-toed from the corner of his mouth and, remarkably, he almost laughed; almost.

'Oh very droll, Mrs Hudson, very droll indeed; for a moment there I thought you were serious. Your excellent histrionics completely fooled me; a capital performance, dear lady—capital.'

He wanted acknowledgement of his expertise in uncovering her ruse. None emerged. She remained serious and continued her astonishing dialogue.

'Originally I thought of conducting tours here at 221B.'

'Tours?!' Holmes slipped back into being amazed and repeating things.

'I thought of calling them, *At home with Holmes*. Visitors could take tea and enjoy the surrounds of this famous sitting-room—all for a fee of course.'

Again he became Mr Unhappy Holmes. 'Enough, madam, cease this nonsensical fantasy. It is inconceivable anyone would ever wish to visit this non-descript Baker Street abode and, if they did, to pay for so doing is preposterous.'

She paid no heed to him or his words. 'So instead I've settled on publishing my memoirs—hence the book. But as I said, not before you have retired and departed London for the countryside.'

Unbelievably, Holmes continued to struggle with the words of his landlady. As he suffered, she shone. In a frantic rear guard action, he tried another tack.

'Mrs Hudson, I strongly advise caution before proceeding with this venture.'

'I agree, sir, which is why I intend asking Dr Watson for advice. Surely he must know the editor of *The Strand Magazine*.'

The detective failed to contain his rising disquiet. He'd dealt with a venomous snake, a ferocious hound, a murderous professor, and countless other dangers and criminals. Many of his foes were desperate, conniving adversaries. Now his foe was the tea-lady. Surely a misguided, elderly female would be child's play. He tried persuasion.

'Madam, writing is a craft requiring knowledge and expertise, both of which I fear you lack. And you do not deserve the indignity of having some bumbling editor returning your work unread.'

'But I haven't sent it yet.'

'Dr Watson wrote his reports based on first-hand experience. He stood by my side, observing, helping me solve the cases.'

'And I too have been by your side, observing your many failures.'

The tension edged higher. Holmes tried a change of subject and waxed lyrical. 'I would have been lost without my Boswell.'

'But didn't you once say most of Dr Watson's conclusions were erroneous?'

In tennis parlance, the landlady's passing shot left Holmes flat-footed. On song, she played a blinder leaving the great man rattled. He had no choice; 'twas time to return fire with fire.

'Mrs Hudson, in the many long years I have lived beneath your roof, I have never once known you to comment on anything of significance. When occasionally performing such menial tasks as housekeeper, cook and receptionist, you have displayed admirable qualities. And as a woman, you are ideally qualified for the execution of domestic duties in which wit and wisdom play no part whatsoever.'

'I see you're still struggling with the concept of flattery, sir.'

Holmes' voice took on a tinge of steel. 'Mrs Hudson, you cannot make bricks without straw. A writer needs reliable research material and your feeble, fading memory is simply not enough.'

'I agree, sir.'

That pleased the detective who inwardly sighed with relief. More fool him. 'Well thank heavens for that.'

From the pocket of her apron she produced a battered book. 'And that is why I've kept this scrap book.' She placed it on the table beside her manuscript as Holmes stumbled into silence.

It is fair to say he was on the ropes, his every thrust parried with ease by the woman who, until now, had played the role of a bit player in the glittering career of the famous detective.

He whispered, 'A scrap book?'

She opened the book. 'You gave me the idea, Mr Holmes.' She indicated various items. 'Like you, I collect newspaper articles, photographs, letters and more about you and your cases. I've used these items as the basis of my book. Would you care to peruse my scrapbook, my manuscript, or both?'

Holmes tapped his pipe against the grate. 'Neither thank you; I have my packing to complete.'

Rattled, Holmes placed various items in a bag with certainly no method in his angry madness. Mrs Hudson sat and observed. Eventually he stopped and glared at her.

'It's late, madam. I recommend you retire.'

'I would like your advice, Mr Holmes.'

'Can you not see I am busy?'

'Perhaps one question, if I may.' He hesitated and she grabbed her chance. 'Do you think it's possible my book can correct *all* the mistakes made by you and the good doctor?'

Holmes froze, unsure what had happened or was happening. Could this be some terrible dream? This woman, always an understudy, a minor character in the masterpiece of his adventure-packed life, now stood centre-stage, in the limelight, displaying the artistic skills of a seasoned trouper. How on Earth should he react? Before he decided, Mrs Hudson gestured and, as if under her power, he sat.

'I warn you, madam, I am not in the mood for trifles.'

'But there is nothing so important as trifles, Mr Holmes.'

In shock, he stared at her with a mixture of surprise and disdain. Now his own words were being thrown back at him.

He spoke through gritted teeth. 'Kindly proceed.'

She read from her notes. 'You have claimed one of your grandmothers is a sister of the French painter Vernet.'

'She is.'

'But there are several French painters called Vernet.' Holmes swallowed. 'One artistic Monsieur Vernet fathered 22 children, four of whom were well-known painters.'

He scrambled a reply. 'What I have said is absolutely true.'

'Yes, but confusing. Your description is akin to me saying my grandfather was an Irishman called Murphy.'

He returned to muttering. 'Yes, yes, I take your point.'

'Or my German grandmother was a Frau Schmidt from Berlin.'

Holmes snapped his reply. 'All right! I believe my great-uncle to be Emile Jean Horace Vernet born in 1789. He painted gentlemen engaged in boxing and fencing, which, incidentally, were *my* sporting interests many years ago. Now, is that all?' He stood.

'Is that all? Oh Mr Holmes, you cannot be serious.' She indicated her manuscript and clippings. 'I've barely begun, sir. You and Dr Watson have bequeathed such a treasure trove of anomalies, my book will probably run to a second volume.'

His mouth opened and remained so. He sat.

'I've studied all your cases beginning from your first, *The Study in Scarlet*.'

'Ha,' scoffed the detective, enjoying a blissful change of mood, and grasping a tiny portion of the moral high ground. 'I fear, madam, your literary adventure is a waste of time. It is not *The* Study but rather *A Study in Scarlet*.'

Mrs Hudson scribbled a note remaining quietly enthusiastic.

'Thank you, Mr Holmes. Attention to detail is so important. Now are you aware Dr Watson has made many mistakes in his written accounts of your work?'

Holmes dipped into his well of indignation. 'I know no such thing.'

'He wrote that when fighting in Afghanistan he was struck in the shoulder by a Jezail bullet.'

'He did venture to Afghanistan where he was indeed injured.'

'Yes but later he referred to the same wound being in his leg.' A pause began. 'I can give you proof in the published cases.'

The detective assumed an air of superiority. 'Alas, madam, you have made an elementary mistake.' Mrs Hudson frowned. Her vehicle veered off the road; her second error. She'd fired one of her best shots which missed—badly. Was her project doomed to fail?

'Watson did suffer a wound in battle,' said Holmes, who stood and moved beside his chair. 'He crouched like so, high above the enemy.' Holmes bent to demonstrate Watson's situation, and indicated parts of his body as he explained. 'The bullet struck his leg here, passing through to his shoulder, here.'

Mrs Hudson gulped. 'Oh dear,' she said, despondent at having her evidence destroyed with such simplicity. Sadness touched her heart.

'Thank you, Mr Holmes. Perhaps my book needs some revision before being presented to the world.' She gathered her belongings. 'I'll leave you in peace,' she said heading for the door.

He called. 'Mrs Hudson.'

She turned and was shocked to see her tenant bent double. His face showed agony and she hurried towards him placing her papers on the table.

'Oh, Mr Holmes, is it your rheumatism again.'

'No, madam, I often pose like this of an evening.'

She ignored his sarcasm and prepared to assist. 'Allow me to help, Mr Holmes.'

'If you would be so kind,' he said, forcing the beginning of a smile. It didn't bloom.

She paused. 'Ah, where should I place my hands?'

Holmes endured serious pain. 'Oh for pity's sake, woman—place them anywhere.'

The landlady remained uncertain but determined. 'Mr Holmes, I would prefer *some*where.'

'Well *some*where then. But please, help un-bend me.'

She stood in front of him, placed her hands on his shoulders, paused then heaved, well, strained. He joined the action, stifled a scream, straightened then collapsed in a chair. He stared at her and she stared back. He remained mute but his eyes, his whole face dared her to leave.

Chapter 2

AS MRS HUDSON FLUMMOXED her famous tenant, elsewhere in London, a group of professional gentlemen gathered in the luxurious Carlton Hotel on the corner of the Haymarket and Pall Mall. In post-Victorian London, clubbing for many chaps was de rigeur. The new club, initially called *The Murder Club,* drew members interested in crime, law, medicine, theatre and writing. The original name didn't stick and it became and remains the *Crimes Club.*

On certain Sunday evenings, members came to dine, converse, amuse and learn from one another. The best raconteurs inspired, educated and entertained. Of course there was gossip—males can rival the fairer sex in that area—but examination of a crime was what set tongues wagging. The analysis of crimes, both real and fictional, fascinated members.

The hotel was run by one Monsieur César Ritz, a Swiss hotelier from humble origins whose name lives on in the hotels he managed in Paris and London. M. Ritz worked at London's Savoy Hotel but moved across town when The Carlton opened its doors. He pinched the chef from The Savoy, a Frenchman, Monsieur Georges Auguste Escoffier, who knew a thing or five about sauces, and was known as "the king of chefs and the chef of kings". This meant the fine dining for members of the *Crimes Club* was very fine indeed, and in truth, a smidgeon above superb.

Membership was restricted. The *Crimes Club* began when a few friends suggested regular meetings with like-minded fellows might be interesting and beneficial. It was networking about a century before the word popped into the vernacular.

Members included doctors and lawyers with some being both. Many were Oxford chaps. Many dabbled in writing be that journalism, editing, non-fiction and/or fiction. Several were amateur sleuths. In time, real detectives in the form of retired police officers joined the club. Most members pursued an interest in theatre be that writing, reviewing, even performing, and definitely as theatregoers and so having Her Majesty's next door proved handy.

But who were some of the members of the *Crimes Club* in its early years? Certainly being a gentleman was a given.

Henry Irving, son of the great thespian, Sir Henry Irving, was fascinated by all things criminal. Bertram Fletcher Robinson loved a mystery and one in particular involving the footprints of a gigantic hound. Sadly Robinson died not long after the formation of the club. Members would have discussed a fascinating topic had they been able to see into the future when some bright spark reckoned Robinson was poisoned by a chum, another member of the *Crimes Club*, and the bright spark wanted Robinson's remains exhumed to prove the nonsensical claim. The exhumation request was sensibly denied.

George R. Sims, a sort of English Mark Twain, supported societal reform penning the ballad, *"It was Christmas Day in the workhouse"*.

A. E. W. Mason, known to Club members as Alf, wrote the novel *The Four Feathers* and proved a dab hand at spying and fast bowling. Ingleby Oddie changed careers being a naval surgeon, a barrister and, as a coroner, oversaw some 30,000 cases. Professor John Churton Collins, a bookish man with a photographic memory, suffered a tragic death in a ditch which read like a scene from a penny dreadful.

Max Pemberton, the dandy with waistcoats and a moustache to entertain, won a Rowing Blue at Cambridge and picked up a law degree in-between riding to hounds. His novels were hits. Arthur Lambton was given out at Lord's. He fell over in the Members' Stand and died from his injuries. He lived as a tax collector, prolific writer and spy catcher for MI5. William Le Queux could be labelled an ink thief. He made busy writers appear lazy. He interviewed murderers, wrote a collection of short stories under the title *The Crimes Club*, and was arguably the world's greatest amateur spy.

These were some of the members who met in The Carlton Hotel in the early years of the 20th century. There were others, one of whom needs no introduction. None of the aforementioned fellows enjoyed the worldwide popularity of a certain GP turned novelist. Sir Arthur Conan Doyle penned sixty tales about the consulting detective, Mr Sherlock Holmes, which were already massively successful and destined for even greater recognition when the club began.

When Doyle joined the *Crimes Club*, Holmes was someone his creator disliked, hated even. Doyle killed the detective only to revive him due to a public outcry. At the time, little did both men know they were about to face a challenge which threatened their sanity.

As Sir Arthur enjoyed a post-dinner brandy and the conversation of like-minded fellows, he had no idea that across London, his soon-to-be retired creation, Sherlock Holmes, wallowed in despair. A demure, inconspicuous landlady had dropped a literary bombshell.

'What news of Mr Holmes, Doyle?' asked Le Queux, himself a writer of detective stories.

'Retired and this time for good,' replied Doyle.

Other members teased him. 'You said that last time, old man,' said Mason. 'You killed the poor blighter and infuriated half of London.'

'Half of Britain,' corrected Pemberton. Members laughed.

'Did you know,' replied Doyle, 'after *The Adventure of the Final Problem*, I was in the High Street when a dear old biddy accosted me with her umbrella?' Fellow diners laughed. True tales were the best.

Doyle imitated the elderly woman using a quavery voice, and waving a clenched fist as he spoke. 'You killed Sherlock Holmes!'

A volley of laughter filled the room. As it settled a gentle knock occurred, the door opened and the chef de cuisine entered. His English was poor and various Francophile members assisted.

'Forgive this intrusion, gentlemen,' said Monsieur Escoffier. 'I trust everything is to your satisfaction.'

Members spoke as one and with enthusiasm. The company was first-class but having a meal prepared by one of the world's greatest chefs was the finest of icing on the finest of cakes.

'Excellent.' M. Escoffier smiled, bowed and turned to leave.

'Ah Monsieur, kindly remain, s'il vous plait.' The chef waited. 'Is it true you have prepared dishes for royalty?' asked Alf Mason.

'Oui; I 'ave for the Prince of Wales and Kaiser Wilhelm II.'

'Then, if I may, a question concerning your knowledge of famous people.' The chef struggled to smile. *What could this possibly mean?*

'Have you met and what do you know of the King of Bohemia?'

M. Escoffier's face relaxed. 'I am sure I 'ave cooked for His Majesty. And I 'ave 'eard a rumour that once the King was saved from a rather delicate situation thanks to the bravery and skill of the world-famous detective, Mr Sherlock 'olmes.'

Members laughed, clapped and one even slapped the table, his other hand clutching a cigar. Sir Arthur felt proud but with a tinge of uncertainty. *Will I ever be rid of that damn detective?*

Mason turned to Doyle. 'You might take note of your friend's popularity, Doyle. Mr Holmes is a damn fine fellow.'

'Hear, hear,' bounced around the room with more laughter, and the chef de cuisine left. Doyle put on a brave face. The hubbub settled.

'Gentlemen,' said Lambton, 'I know it is many years since the atrocities in Whitechapel, but I have arranged a tour of the Ripper murder sites if anyone is interested.'

Replies were immediate, supportive and enthusiastic.

'Through a friend,' continued Lambton, 'I have met Detective Inspector Fred Wensley of Scotland Yard.'

'Fine fellow,' said Irving.

'Absolutely first-rate,' added Doyle.

'He's offered to lead the excursion but requested it remain a secret. We know how the press thrive on anything salacious and having members of the *Crimes Club* poking around Whitechapel could spark headlines to embarrass us all.'

'Damn,' said Pemberton. 'I could pen a ripping article for *Chums*.

Members laughed. Many murmured their pleasure at the prospect of the excursion. 'I'll confirm the details now I know we're all keen to be involved,' said Lambton.

Glasses were raised and members of the *Crimes Club* finished another damn fine function.

Chapter 3

MRS HUDSON CHOSE TO REMAIN. Her famous tenant suffered and two things made his situation worse. He would soon leave London to live alone in the English countryside. *Who would straighten Sherlock in Sussex?* And furthermore, the great man now knew his once trusted landlady had compiled a list of his and Dr Watson's many failures. The cat was out of the bag but kindness, at least from one person in the room, remained available.

'Let me get you a cup of tea, Mr Holmes.' She fussed. He accepted the tea with a singular lack of gratitude. She moved to the opposite chair beside the fireplace and sat. This was noteworthy bordering on unbelievable because such an event had never happened before tonight. The embers faded in the grate in the clock-ticking room. A single lamp cast an eerie glow. Finally the detective spoke without making eye contact with his landlady.

'It has been a remarkable evening, Mrs Hudson.'

'I apologise for getting the title of your first case wrong, Mr Holmes.'

'A mere trifle, madam,' he muttered then stopped. They glanced at one another. Holmes again mentioned trifles only this time she didn't take advantage of his choice of word.

After a long pause she continued. 'I hoped you'd be pleased with my literary endeavours.' He grunted. 'May I ask if you are more upset at my revealing your faults or at my hitherto hidden qualities as an articulate woman with a mind of her own?'

If Holmes felt intimidated at some of his landlady's previous questions, this latest interrogative knocked him for six. His response became an admission of failure. Or did it?

'I have nothing further to add, Mrs Hudson. You have clearly made up your mind to tell all and nothing I can say or do will remove your ambition, and, may I say, your prejudice.'

She remembered a key point.

'Oh do please forgive me, Mr Holmes. I should have explained that all the money I earn from the sale of my book will go to the *Society for the Rescue of Young Women and Children.*'

Holmes remained silent. She continued.

'I believe you would support such a gesture and hope you can help me refine my memoir.'

'Oh, so now you're asking me to *write* the book.'

'No, no, no. I simply ask if you will correct any errors.'

'You want me to correct your errors of my errors?'

'Well your errors do exist, Mr Holmes.'

'So you keep saying.'

The mood fluctuated. The anger Holmes displayed before, now became a sort of masochistic fascination. Another pause lingered. She tried a new tack.

'There is your reputation to consider, Mr Holmes.' His blood pressure rose. 'By tactfully explaining your miscalculations, ignorance and possible fraud, the world will discover the human side of the world's greatest detective. You will be loved even more and *by* more.'

This sincere praise and well-made point made matters worse. Holmes resumed seething. His mind spun. It wasn't the accusations so much as their source.

According to the downstairs domestic, I'm a fraudster.

'As you clearly have a modicum of intelligence, madam, I assume you are aware of the laws pertaining to libel.'

'I am, sir, and believe truth will be my defence.' Her retort rocked the sleuth. 'May I present the case for the prosecution?'

The last time he breathed as he did now occurred when he faced a certain professor of mathematics on a narrow pathway beside a Swiss waterfall. His eyes dared her to speak. She did.

'Mr Holmes, you claim to be the author of a monograph on the polyphonic motets of the Franco-Flemish composer, Orlande de Lassus.'

'I claim to be because I *am* that author.'

'Well, sir, I have been to every music retailer in London, and searched the libraries and museums of this great metropolis, and failed to find even a trace of your literary offering. Furthermore, not a single retailer, librarian or curator has even *heard* of your work.'

'You would call me a liar?'

'I merely report the facts. There is nothing like first-hand evidence.'

Hearing his own words thrown back at him pushed Holmes into action. He moved to the table, covered in a jumble of yet-to-be-packed material, and searched.

'Madam, I shall prove my claim by finding the monograph to which you refer.' He lifted, sifted and shifted and, as he did, his anger increased. 'I know it's here somewhere; it has to be.'

'Mr Holmes, even if you were to summon Dr "Lazarus" Livingstone from his Westminster resting place, even he could never discover the source of your manuscript in this, your chaotic clutter. I submit, sir, you have claimed authorship of a non-existent document.'

He kept searching. 'It's here. I know it's here.' Holmes tossed some books back on the table. 'I'll find it later,' he snorted.

'May we move from wrongful attribution to basic fraud?' Holmes froze as dread took hold of his mind and body. His landlady, despite the odd stumble, landed some telling blows. And what made things even worse was the lack of warning. This "performance" came out of nowhere, exploded, and worse still, his mainly mute "servant" was on the front foot and winning.

'Fraud?' he snapped.

'The matter concerns tobacco ash.'

'Ah, yes. I have indeed written a monograph on the ash produced by 140 different varieties of pipe, cigar and cigarette tobacco.' He fired a sarcastic question. 'Have you found that particular document?'

'I've not been bothered.' Holmes clenched his fists. 'This time the existence of your work is not an issue. This time we consider the truth of your claims.'

We? Who's we? Holmes glared at his landlady. 'The *truth* you say?'

'When you published your findings, the scientific world was not as advanced as it is today.'

Her words carried a ring of authority and, such was his shock, a feather might well have flattened him. The landlady pressed her case.

'Today, scientists believe it's impossible to positively distinguish one tobacco ash from another.' His eyes widened. 'Apparently the aromas are unique and the ash varies according to the rate at which it is smoked. But defining ash, as you claim, is simply not possible.'

Sherlock's night spiralled towards an abyss. He paid Mrs Hudson the ultimate compliment by questioning her statement.

'A powerful claim, madam, but are you sure of your facts?'

She made eye contact to deliver her knockout punch.

'I am, sir, having been blessed with such a wonderful teacher. I never guess. It is a shocking habit—destructive to the logical faculty.'

The world's greatest consulting detective stood gobsmacked. The answer to his probing question was answered with the words of Sherlock Holmes himself—his reply, incoherent.

'I'm sorry, Mr Holmes, I missed what you said.'

Surely the great man had not surrended? 'Would you agree, madam, attacking a detective in his autumnal years is indeed a tad cruel?' This sounded like a concession. It *was* a concession. He applied for the sympathy vote. Who would have guessed that?

'Perhaps, but many of your elementary errors were made in your prime.'

'Oh?' queried Holmes with both regret and anxiety. *What's next?*

'I am puzzled when, in *The Adventure of Blue Peter*, you spent ...

'*Black*,' snapped Holmes, '*The Adventure of <u>Black</u> Peter*.'

Mrs Hudson scribbled a note. 'Thank you, Mr Holmes.' With barely a pause she continued. 'I cannot understand why you spent three days sending telegrams to Scotland.'

Holmes shook his head. In deep water and struggling to survive, a straw floated towards him. He grasped at it. Finally he hoped to return to the game; finally a question which encapsulated the rampant ignorance of his landlady. Thank goodness, she was fallible after all.

'Madam, it is a capital mistake to theorize before one has data. I simply sought information about ships and their masters in order to solve the case. They were my proven methods.' Holmes sniffed and gloated.

'Yes but why send telegrams when a telephone stood across the road?' Holmes stopped gloating. 'You could have wrapped up the case in hours, possibly even minutes.'

Air rushed to escape the detective's body. A soft request emanated from his lips. 'Are you sure a telephone stood across the road?'

'Dr Watson referred to it in another case.'

Holmes scrambled for a foothold en route to the moral high ground—the now very low, moral high ground.

'Ah, well there you have it. Watson's reports are not to be wholly trusted.'

'At last, Mr Holmes, there is something upon which we may agree.' He breathed a little easier. The pressure shifted to his colleague. Mrs Hudson referred to her notes and fired a new question.

'Tell me, please, which of the following is the odd one out—snake, jellyfish, butterfly and orchid?'

Holmes replied without hesitation. 'Clearly the latter; three are animal whereas the orchid is a plant.'

'Your answer is partly correct, sir.' Holmes feared her explanation. 'There is no odd one out because each of the four items is a Watsonian gaffe. I regret to say your friend and colleague made many mistakes.'

Holmes felt tempted to say that Watson leaving his landlady's gaff was not a gaffe, but, on the contrary clearly a brilliant move.

Pity I didn't do likewise.

Mrs Hudson elaborated. 'I refer to the snake in *The Adventure of the Speckled Band*, the jellyfish in *The Adventure of the Lion's Mane*, and the butterfly and orchid in *The Hound of the Baskervilles*.'

'And so now we proceed to your nit picking par excellence.'

She ignored his sarcasm. 'It is highly unlikely a swamp-adder would respond to a whistle, drink milk or kill a human in a trice.'

Holmes felt a new sensation—a dislike for his faithful landlady.

'Well let's fetch that breed of snake, Mrs Hudson, and you can pretend to be Mr Roylott.'

'*Doctor* Roylott,' she corrected him with barely disguised glee. 'And if you identified the snake correctly as a swamp-adder, then it came from Africa, not India.' Holmes gulped at the geographic schoolboy howler. 'Furthermore, you would have us believe pets, a cheetah and a baboon, were free to wander the grounds restrained by a fence so low a cockroach could step over it.'

Holmes drifted towards the fuming and exploding stage.

'Next, Dr Watson reports on a death by jellyfish sting.'

'Quite painful I'm told,' replied the hapless Holmes, scrambling to stay in the game.

'But a jellyfish floats in the sea making it almost impossible to be stood upon, and besides, the sting from a *Cyanea* jellyfish is unlikely to cause serious injury, let alone death.'

The detective floundered in the sea as a shark, in the form of his landlady with her powerful reasoning, encircled him. She swam ever closer.

'The *Chequered Skipper* butterfly has never been seen in Devonshire, and the *Mare's Tail* orchid flowers in mid-summer, yet Dr Watson places both squarely on Dartmoor in mid-September.'

Holmes lost the plot and snapped. 'So Mrs Hudson, were you there? Did you skirt treacherous mires and oozing black bogs?'

'No, Mr Holmes.'

'Were you living rough upon the moor? Amidst the swirling mists, did you confront the howling beast and murderous madman? Well?'

'You know very well I didn't, Mr Holmes.'

'We *all* know, madam. We *all* know you were tucked up nice and warm here in dear old Baker Street; comfy chair, cheery fire, and steaming cup of cocoa.'

'Actually I too had much to do, Mr Holmes.'

He sneered. 'Oh yes, doing what?'

'Why, refining my memoir preparing for this very conversation.'

Bang! Mrs Hudson landed a telling blow. Holmes fell back against the ropes, his eyes puffy and closed from her stinging blows. She advanced for the kill.

'But probably my most distressing discovery, Mr Holmes, concerns your slapdash approach to detail.'

Wow! Talk about a coup de grâce. His face matched the ash in the grate as he spoke in a sort of growl. 'I have been called many things, madam, but never slapdash.'

'Many times I have heard you refer to the publication, *Bradshaw's Railway Companion.*'

His voice sounded proud, even reverent. 'It is my bible.'

'Then why sir; in 1899, in *The Boscombe Valley Mystery,* did you send a telegram to Dr Watson asking him to meet you at Paddington Station in time to catch the 11.15 train?'

Holmes shook his head. Surely the woman has gone too far.

'I confess to being confused, Mrs Hudson. What on Earth has my perfectly logical telegram got to do with me supposedly being slapdash?'

'Check your beloved *Bradshaw,* Mr Holmes. In 1899 there *was* no train at 11.15.'

Smack! This latest claim flattened the professional who became speechless. She attacked with a quote; his words.

'Tut, tut, my dear sir, you must really pay attention to these details.'

Mrs Hudson kept using the words of Sherlock Holmes to attack Sherlock Holmes. It proved a brilliant tactic. As Holmes prepared to throw in the towel, to admit his career needed a serious reappraisal, a resounding knock sounded. That sound became the timekeeper's bell as the metaphorical referee stepped in to help Holmes hang on.

Someone stood outside the Baker Street front door.

Chapter 4

'OH MISTER HOLMES, who can it be at this time of night?' asked a concerned Mrs Hudson. The door-knocking continued.

'Send them away. Ignore them. I have retired. Sherlock Holmes is dead.' After Mrs Hudson's battering routine, he felt like death.

She departed, worried, shaking her head. Alone, the detective groaned. Wide awake, he endured a nightmare. Bad news is worse when it's unexpected. Had Mrs Hudson been a spy, a sleeper, her awakening proved to be pitch perfect—it was never suspected and packed a powerful and potentially devastating impact. Her data collection was brilliant and her timing and delivery even more so.

Downstairs, the door knocking continued. Over the last two decades, the landlady opened the door of this Baker Street abode countless times, and to all manner of people. She greeted rich, poor, young, old, male, female, desperate and defeated, of different races and religions including none. She met royalty and ratbags; the lot. But now, fresh from a remarkable "encounter" with her famous tenant, with the hour late and the knocking ever more insistent, the elderly woman felt a twinge of concern as she descended the stairs wondering who demanded entrance. Taking a deep breath, she opened the door and relief flooded her body.

'Dr Watson,' she exclaimed as her former tenant stood smiling on the doorstep. 'Good evening, sir. Do come in.'

'Good evening, Mrs Hudson and please forgive my calling at such an inhospitable hour.' She took his hat, gloves and cane. 'I trust the great man has not retired, either to bed or to Sussex.'

'He is still here and still up, but I fear his health is not the best.'

'Ah, the dreaded rheumatism,' said the medical man, and indicated a small package. 'I have the perfect remedy, Mrs Hudson—a single malt from the country of my birth.'

She smiled as they climbed the seventeen stairs at a rate much slower than when Holmes and Watson first arrived in this residence all those years ago. She spoke quietly and he followed suit.

'You should be aware, Doctor, Mr Holmes has not yet warmed to his retirement decision.'

'Oh?'

'He's been packing for days but slowly, as I suspect he wants to stay. He seems bored with the whole idea of giving up work.'

'Oh dear. We know he hated being bored, and when left without a case, how he fell into a certain bad habit.' They stopped.

'I think you mean bad habits, plural, Dr Watson.'

He nodded. 'Perhaps he fears retirement will not provide the stimulus a case would offer. I'll cheer him up.' He smiled to lift the depressing mood; as warm as when he first set foot in Baker Street.

They resumed their ascent until two-thirds of the way up she stopped, as much to gather her breath as to enquire. 'I'm so sorry, Doctor. How are you and your good lady wife?' She put a hand to her face, embarrassed. 'Oh, forgive me, I've forgotten your wife's name.'

Watson smiled. 'You're not alone, dear lady. Many people ask such a question, and I avoid embarrassing slips by sticking to "My dear" and "Mrs Watson".

Mrs Hudson wondered how her former tenant would react to her literary creation. He was as much involved as Mr Holmes. She felt a certain warmth for John Watson. Mr Holmes was the snappy, brash and eccentric side of the partnership; Dr Watson the softer, kinder, the more old-school-chum side. They reached the landing where Watson placed a hand on Mrs Hudson's arm and whispered.

'I say, why not announce me as a possible client with a most intriguing mystery.'

Mrs Hudson stifled her reaction. 'Oh I don't think so, Doctor. Mr Holmes is in somewhat of a peculiar mood.'

'When is he not?' The landlady offered a weak smile and Watson took a different tack. 'Then don't announce me and I'll give the fellow a grand surprise.'

Dr Watson's boyish grin pushed Mrs Hudson to reluctantly agree. She stopped at the sitting-room door, looked back at the grinning visitor, and then tapped lightly. She entered and despaired. Holmes sat slumped in his chair by the fire staring at the grate.

'Mr Holmes, there is someone to see you.'

He dismissed her. 'Good night, Mrs Hudson.'

She moved closer and spoke with warmth. 'I think you should receive this visitor, Mr Holmes.'

He paused, stood, and then walked past her to the door. Looking back at his landlady, he pointed and pointedly said, 'Good night, Mrs Hudson.'

She froze. As Holmes raised his voice to repeat the command, the visitor made his entrance.

'And a very good evening to you, kind sir.'

Watson beamed and his friend's anger melted at the sight and sound of his friend and companion.

'Watson,' exclaimed Holmes, and the two men greeted one another with feeling.

Watson was ebullient. 'My dear chap, I could not allow you to retire without saying goodbye in person.'

'Too kind, Watson, you are too kind.'

The doctor indicated his gift. 'I've brought a wee drop to help us celebrate the old days.' Watson turned to the statuesque landlady. 'Glasses, if you please, Mrs Hudson.' She nodded and moved to the sideboard. 'And let us have *three* glasses. We must *all* celebrate this momentous occasion together.'

'Oh I don't think so, Dr Watson,' she said.

'Come now, madam. You were here when Holmes and I first met. You've been here ever since, and you are the one person who should help us honour our friendship. Tell her, Holmes.'

The pause felt awkward and the silence loud. Watson looked at his friend then at Mrs Hudson. Despite his longstanding ability to miss even the most obvious of clues, Watson knew something was amiss.

Holmes spoke in a soft but determined voice. 'The hour is late, Watson. We should not detain Mrs Hudson.'

Being a gentleman, Watson agreed but with a heavy heart. He said nothing. Mrs Hudson placed two glasses on the table, and picked up her tray.

'Mr Holmes is right, Dr Watson. I'll leave you to reminisce in peace. Goodnight gentlemen.'

Watson moved to the door and helped her depart. 'Goodnight, Mrs Hudson,' he said and turned back to his friend.

'Close it,' whispered Holmes.

Confused, Watson whispered in return. 'Why are we whispering?'

'The door,' hissed Holmes, and Watson obliged. His nerves tingled. Something was afoot and his friendly late-night social call now bubbled with intrigue. Watson reacted true to character.

'I say, old chap; is this necessary? In our long and wonderful partnership, the one constant is dear old Mrs Hudson.'

'She's mad,' said Holmes, sotto voce.

'I know she's never been involved in our cases but ...' Watson gasped. 'What did you say?'

'Stand still,' said Holmes who crept to the door and listened.

'Holmes?' whispered Watson, and fell silent when the detective put a finger to his lips.

Satisfied Mrs Hudson had departed, Holmes returned to his chair by the fire. Watson joined him and the two men sat and stared at one another as they had done for decades. Holmes was never more serious; Watson never more incredulous, although the latter was not an unusual condition for the physician.

'Watson, you will not believe what has happened here tonight.'

The detective's manner and tone were enough to have Watson on edge. The words spoken by Holmes were brimming with danger.

'You have often perplexed me, Holmes, but never more so than at this precise moment.'

'Believe me, Watson; I am as shocked as you. Until an hour ago, we shared the same respect for Mrs Hudson but now I am convinced she has suffered a major nervous breakdown, her mind is disturbed, and the woman, I regret to say, is stark raving mad.'

'Good heavens,' mouthed Watson. 'Has she suffered a stroke? She appeared in good health. Should I call a cab or an ambulance?'

'I fear the matter is so serious, you and your medical colleagues will be of no use whatsoever.'

Watson felt ill. 'I must say, she's disguised her illness very well. Tell me, what are her symptoms?'

Holmes hesitated then, boring his eyes into Watson's, growled. 'She's written a book.'

Watson could not have been more surprised had Holmes revealed some monstrous scandal about the humble septuagenarian. Watson's face screamed shock. He copied Holmes and joined the Repetition Club.

'She's written a book?'

'Proving the woman is clearly insane.'

'They are her symptoms of insanity?'

Holmes nodded. 'Wait till you see the contents.' Watson's heart pumped faster. Fear gripped his chest. A terrifying thought flooded his brain. *Mrs Hudson is not insane. Sherlock Holmes is insane.*

The atmosphere in the room switched to electric. Holmes, clearly distressed about Mrs Hudson's state of mind, shocked Watson. Watson, clearly distressed about his friend's state of mind, carefully began to investigate.

'So Mrs Hudson has written a book. I never would have guessed it.'

Holmes moved to the window through which an assassin once took aim at a dummy believing it to be the detective.

'This is serious, Watson. It's a matter of the greatest importance.'

Throughout their friendship, Watson constantly struggled to follow his friend's intuitive thinking. For years Watson watched first-hand as Holmes unravelled mysteries in which Watson so often failed to discover any relevant clue. Even now, understanding Sherlock Holmes and his methodology continued to evade the good doctor. *What on Earth has happened?* Watson resumed his gentle probing.

'Have you seen this book written by Mrs Hudson?'

'I have, and she read parts of it aloud. It is based on her diary and supportive documents.' He scoffed; 'her scrap book.'

'Her scrap book?'

'There,' pointed Holmes. 'She left her masterpiece on the table.'

Watson looked but the table contained so many items, finding Mrs Hudson's material would require a search party and compass.

'Holmes, are you saying the matter of greatest importance is in fact Mrs Hudson's book?'

'That is precisely what I am saying; as will you when you discover its contents.'

The men stopped speaking. Something significant, possibly momentous, even dangerous, had happened in this sitting-room and Watson was desperate to discover the facts. Even in the most terrifying of situations when working with Holmes, Watson never felt fear as he did now. He battled to disguise his nerves.

In a poor attempt at humour, and as a way of relieving pressure, Watson joked. 'I can't believe Mrs Hudson has taken up detective fiction,' he said.

'Oh it's far worse than detective fiction, my good fellow—the landlady has produced detective *non*-fiction.' Watson gasped. 'The landlady has written her memoir.'

'I say,' remarked Watson, both impressed and worried. 'But surely she has no writing expertise and is, well, she's a woman, Holmes.'

'She plans to reveal my idiosyncrasies to the world.'

'I say,' said Watson, again repeating himself.

'All these years she's hovered in the background, performing her domestic duties, while at the same time surreptitiously making notes about our private lives.'

'Private lives! *Our* private lives!' exclaimed Watson.

'Oh my dear fellow, did I not say? You are as much involved as am I, probably even more so.'

'But ... but that's simply not cricket.'

Holmes filled his pipe. Watson felt an urge to open a window but ignored the impending ghastly tobacco smell such was his interest in Mrs Hudson's tome. Holmes explained.

'She plans to list all the mistakes you published in *The Strand*.'

Watson changed from inquisitive and concerned, to downright alarmed.

'What mistakes? I didn't make mistakes.' They exchanged glances. 'Oh, all right; there may have been the odd, minor one.'

Holmes rebuffed his friend. 'Watson, odd and minor do not apply.'

He flustered; something he did well. 'I don't believe you. Give me even one example—please.'

Holmes paused. He took no pleasure, especially at this their final meeting, to remind his friend of his sloppy prose. 'She went on about your war wound from Afghanistan moving from shoulder to leg.'

Watson's mouth opened. 'But the bullet couldn't move, surely.'

'According to you it did.'

'It must have been my agent or the typesetter or the editor or ...'

'I made up some malarkey about you crouching and the same bullet causing both wounds.'

The sarcasm from Holmes was surpassed by Watson's joy. 'Of course,' he grinned. 'It's a simple explanation of my only mistake.'

'*Only?* Oh Watson, please stop pretending. Your jottings are replete with gaffes galore.'

Watson's bonhomie vanished. 'I say, Holmes, how could you be so cruel, and on our final night in Baker Street?'

'My dear fellow, because you wrote five or six cases in quick succession, always rushing to finish them, you were bound to include errors. That fact is elementary.'

A noisy silence filled the room. What a night. Holmes planned to quietly finish his packing. Watson planned to quietly reminisce. Now both were stunned by some unpublished manuscript which supposedly contained embarrassing, possibly reputation-damaging material. Worse, it came from the most unlikely and unexpected source.

'Holmes, I must examine this manuscript.'

'Don't. You will suffer palpitations.'

'Surely no-one will care to publish the ramblings of an old woman.'

'Who lived under the same roof as the world's best-known consulting detective and his faithful companion and scribe.'

Watson went pale. 'But she has no literary skills, and she's a woman.'

'Irene Adler is a woman.'

True to form, Watson missed the inference but his intention became steadfast. 'Holmes, we must stop this book being published.'

'For once we are as one, Watson, but how?'

'What are her plans?'

'She promised to wait until I retire before contacting the editor of *The Strand Magazine*.'

'*The Strand Magazine!*' exploded Watson. 'She plans to publish in *The Strand?*'

'She asked if I knew the editor and I told her that was your domain.'

Watson appeared confused. '*My* domain? Holmes, I was but the humble scribe. I didn't deal with the editor. I may have met him once but if so, years ago.'

Holmes appeared confused. 'So you sent the cases by post and the editor accepted them, mistakes and all?'

'Good lord, no. I used a literary agent. And if there are any mistakes, which I still very much doubt, we can blame him.'

'But why use a literary agent?'

'Holmes, think; I was an unknown. When I first recorded your cases, I had no reputation or standing in the world of literature. I was hardly Charles Dickens. Editors never approached me requesting my work. Your first case, ah, ...'

'*A Study in Scarlet*,' said Holmes.

Watson nodded. 'I sent it to a number of publications only for it to be rejected every time.'

'Rejected?' asked Holmes with a tinge of anger.

'Some even returned the manuscript unread.'

'Unread!'

'It's true.'

Holmes frowned. His sadness headed towards despair. 'Well how did *The Strand* become involved?'

''They didn't, not then. Your first case started life in a cookbook.'

'What!?' Holmes gasped and raged although he might have raged and gasped. 'Me, the world-famous consulting detective first appeared in a cookbook?'

'Have you heard of Mrs Beeton, a woman who published recipes?'

'Of course.'

'She's long deceased but her husband published a book at Christmas and *A Study in Scarlet* first appeared in *Beeton's Christmas Annual.*'

Sarcasm dripped from the detective's lips. 'What, in-between the recipes for mince pies and turkey stuffing?'

'But afterwards, your other cases were published in *The Strand.*'

The news for Holmes went from bad to worse. He didn't want to retire and to make matters worse, with the discovery of Mrs Hudson's tell-all tales, and the somewhat humble beginnings of the reporting of his first case, the detective's misery plumbed new depths.

'So why did you choose *The Strand?*'

'I didn't.'

Holmes rarely if ever snapped at his Boswell but now, on what was to be their last night together in Baker Street, Holmes came within a whisker of berating his friend.

'Watson, kindly stop speaking in riddles. What did you say to the editor of *The Strand?*'

'Nothing, I told you, I barely knew the man.'

The gleam in the detective's eyes made the room a smidgeon brighter.

'I was never involved in the publication of my writing. My literary agent handled everything.'

This surprised Holmes. He assumed his friend wrote the cases, trotted off to see the editor of *The Strand Magazine* and then, a week or three later, the latest edition would go on sale.

'Your literary agent?' enquired a fascinated Holmes.

'Yes, a chap called Doyle who now adds one of his middle names to his surname. Conan Doyle dealt with the editor.'

'Then we must ensure Mrs Hudson never discovers this Doyle chap. If she does and makes contact, he'll know how to deal with *The Strand* and then the world will discover your mistakes?'

'*My* mistakes. I thought she mentioned yours as well.'

'A few. Now who is this Canon Doyle? A religious man is he?'

'Not Canon, *Conan* Doyle, and he's not religious although decidedly keen on the after-life.'

'More riddles, Watson,' moaned Holmes.

'He's both a student and supporter of spiritualism.'

'A spiritualist!' Holmes groaned, regarding all forms of faith as bunkum. 'He *definitely* can't be trusted.'

'He's a Scot, a retired doctor I met through a medical chum. The fellow's a writer and has penned a few historical novels in the hope of becoming the next Walter Scott.'

'And is he?'

'Is he what?'

'The next Walter Scott?'

'Hardly; I can't even name one of his historical novels. I think that's why he became a literary agent.'

The mood turned sombre, no, more sombre. The men fell silent. Confusion reigned. Were they disappointed Mrs Hudson collected anecdotes of their private lives and made a list of their errors, or that she planned to publish same, or both? *Disappointed* became a mild description of their mood.

The fire in the hearth died. The lamp provided a soft light. Watson opened his bottle of single malt and poured two measures. The friends stood in the quiet sitting-room. Holmes raised his glass.

'To us,' he toasted. Their glasses clinked.

'To us,' responded Watson.

The clock ticked, and the sound of a lone motor vehicle, one of a growing number in the country, approached then faded into the night. Neither man knew that one of the first car owners and drivers in Britain worked as a literary agent; Sir Arthur Conan Doyle.

In the silence, a question dominated the minds of Sherlock Holmes and John H. Watson. Would the memoirs of the hitherto non-descript landlady ever see the light of day?

Chapter 5

AS HOLMES AND WATSON discussed Mrs Hudson's literary efforts, the lady herself found sleep elusive. Revealing her secret hobby to the famous tenant, and seeing his reaction, set fire to her nerves. She worried too about any discussion between Mr Holmes and Dr Watson.

Did they discuss my book? Of course they did? What happened?

She woke the next morning still thinking about her memoir then hurried to bathe and dress. Her brain buzzed.

Is Mr Holmes here? Has he read my manuscript? What now?

She tapped on the sitting-room door. Silence. She tapped again. Quietly, she opened the door.

'Mr Holmes?'

The empty room remained the same as when she left it last night; a recently-used battlefield with the detritus of war everywhere. She moved to the messy table and spied her manuscript and scrapbook. Relief flooded her body. Fearing the imminent arrival of her famous tenant, she gathered her property and left.

In her room, she pondered the situation. Another "discussion" with Mr Holmes didn't appeal. If he again became short and sarcastic, another dose of his "medicine" would hardly be fun and benefit no-one. Criticising someone she long respected hurt both parties.

She worried. *Did Mr Holmes and Dr Watson examine all my writing and in detail? If so, were they upset, even angry?* Many thoughts whirred inside her head with one in particular.

Should I drop the whole thing and destroy my manuscript?

She made a decision, placed her manuscript in her shopping basket, put on her hat and coat, and slipped out the front door.

She left before a visitor arrived at 221B Baker Street. Dr John H. Watson returned, knocked and got more than he bargained for.

Now that he knew about Mrs Hudson's shenanigans, Watson wasn't sure how he should greet the woman. She had not only written a book, in itself, he believed, a remarkable achievement for a woman, but one which castigated his chronicles. According to the landlady, there were mistakes aplenty, and she listed them all. Watson struggled to grasp the situation.

Why would she even <u>think</u> about doing such a thing? I have always behaved as a perfect gentleman to all women, and most certainly to Mrs Hudson. Yes, I admit, I sometimes forget the name of my current wife but a chap can't always be expected to be on top of his game.

He heard movement from inside and pondered his first words. "Good morning, Mrs Hudson," or "How do you do, Mrs Hudson". He said neither because the door opened to reveal a male person.

'Holmes!' spluttered Watson.

'She's gone,' said the detective who turned and headed upstairs.

Watson closed the door and followed his friend to the war zone still doubling as the sitting-room. Holmes stood by a window, staring down into Baker Street.

'What do you mean, she's gone?' asked Watson.

'And she's taken her manuscript and scrapbook.'

Watson surveyed the table where the aforementioned documents once resided. Despite the mess, he could see they were missing.

'I rose early and went to see my brother for advice.'

Watson gasped again. 'You called on Mycroft because of Mrs Hudson's scribbling?'

Holmes flared. 'Last night, after you left, I examined in detail more of her scribbling as you call it, and I can assure you, Watson, if that material ever becomes public, our reputations will be traduced.'

'Really, Holmes, is it that bad?'

'Worse. Your basic errors are numerous, and my ability to perform the simplest of tasks is seriously called into question. Apparently I spent days seeking information by telegram when I could have used the telephone across the road.'

'That doesn't sound like you. Are you sure?'

The replies from Holmes kept getting louder. 'Of course I'm sure, and you should know, you wrote it, thus informing the world of my stupidity.'

Goodness. Holmes lost it, and Watson now regretted returning to Baker Street. Last night was unsettling, unpleasant even, and coming to see Holmes again did not appeal. He should have stayed away. But come he did and the change in his friend left Watson anxious.

Holmes always tackled problems with confidence. Nothing proved too difficult for the thinker, the detective with the deductive mind and the determination to overcome any difficulty. Now, his reason fled; so too inspiration. Holmes allowed fear and anger to control his actions. This was a first for Watson who so wanted to help his friend.

'I'm afraid I don't share your concern, Holmes.'

The detective paced the room, tricky with so many half-filled bags and boxes to negotiate.

'When I returned from my visit to Mycroft, Mrs Hudson was missing along with her documents.'

Watson gave a simple explanation. 'She may be shopping, Holmes, fetching something for your final supper.'

The doctor winced at his choice of words not helped by the glare from his friend who barked. 'Does she need her manuscript to visit the butcher?' He mimicked the landlady. 'A pound of sausages, Mr Wilson, and did you hear about the latest gaffes from Messieurs Holmes and Watson?' Watson winced again. 'We'll be the butt of jokes all along the High Street.'

'Surely not.'

'We'll be mocked in every High Street, sitting-room and pub.'

The sounds in the room consisted of a ticking clock and heavy breathing. Watson tried again to help his friend.

'Was your brother helpful?'

'Hardly; he prattled on about the Bern Convention.'

Dr Ignorance paused, his Scottish ancestry teasing his memory. 'I've not heard of The Burns Convention? Is there a special event to celebrate wee Rabbie?'

The detective snapped again. 'Not Burns the poet; Bern the city in Switzerland.'

'Holmes, I have no idea what you are talking about.'

'Copyright. In 1886, several countries, including Britain, agreed to protect the ownership of creative material such as music and literature. There are laws now concerning works of art. Before these laws, people like Dickens, and Gilbert and Sullivan, had their work copied and sold or performed without the creators receiving a penny.'

Watson still required further explanation. 'I'm afraid I don't see how that relates to Mrs Hudson's prose.'

'When you wrote about my cases which appeared in *The Strand*, that writing is now protected by law. My name, your name and even our landlady's name are now protected by copyright. Mrs Hudson cannot publish anything about us without permission.'

For once Watson uttered something relevant and, more to the point, something scary; so scary it caused Holmes to clutch his chest.

'But my writing is not fiction, Holmes. I reported on real cases, the ones you solved. Surely you can't copyright news. And can you copyright the names of real people like us?'

It was a first; a question, *two* questions from Watson to stump Holmes who had no answer. He filled his pipe, sat in front of the fireplace, and considered his latest three-pipe problem.

Mrs Hudson spent years gathering material and writing her manuscript, and ages thinking about if and when she would reveal her project to Mr Holmes. Now the book was written and the tenant told. She decided. I will "begin as I mean to go on".

She would keep her word and not allow publication before Mr Holmes and Dr Watson retired, but an exploratory chat with a publisher seemed wise and fair. So, where to begin?

Her first port of call was *The Strand Magazine,* the publisher of Mr Holmes' cases as notated by Dr Watson. Because of its name, she wrongly assumed the magazine's offices would be in the Strand.

She bought a tuppeny ticket to travel on the Baker Street and Waterloo Railway and alighted at Charing Cross.

Out in the sunshine, she wandered along the Strand searching for a sign, *The Strand Magazine*. She found none so stopped a copy boy.

'Excuse me, young man,' she said. 'Can you direct me to the office of *The Strand Magazine?*'

'Yes, madam. Keep going and Burleigh Street is on your left.'

She thanked the lad and continued. Peeking inside her shopping basket, she checked to see her precious cargo remained safe and sound. In Burleigh Street, she paused outside her destination. Could anyone hear her beating heart? The moment of truth arrived.

Inside the reception area, a young man, Ernest Balfour, worked at a desk. 'Good morning, madam,' he said.

'Good morning,' said the landlady cum budding writer.

'May I be of assistance?'

Producing her carefully wrapped pages, she spoke in a soft but determined voice. 'I have information about Mr Sherlock Holmes and his friend, Dr Watson.'

Interested, the young man stood. 'Information you say?'

'Yes. Over the years I've studied their cases, and observed their behaviour. I've made notes and believe the world should be told.'

'So you're a reader of the Sherlock Holmes' cases?'

'I'm sorry?'

'You've read his adventures when they appeared in *The Strand?*'

'I've read them *before* they appeared in *The Strand.*'

Ernest looked surprised and impressed. *She must be a friend of Sir Arthur*. 'And have you told Sir Arthur about this information?'

For the first time since entering the office, Mrs Hudson hesitated. The name Sir Arthur was new to her. 'I'm afraid I don't understand.'

'Oh, every week, people send us ideas for new Sherlock Holmes' adventures and we forward them to Sir Arthur Conan Doyle.' Ernest turned to see if anyone might enter the office. The coast was clear. He turned back to Mrs Hudson and whispered. 'Actually, we like to give Sir Arthur a gentle push every now and then to see if we can help rekindle his enthusiasm for the magnificent detective.'

'I see,' said Mrs Hudson, who didn't see at all.

'Why don't you post your material to Sir Arthur? I'm sure he'll be delighted to receive it. You never know, one day your information may end up being published in *The Strand*.'

'Really?' asked Mrs Hudson, her spirits lifting.

'Yes, the best person for advice on Mr Holmes and Dr Watson is Sir Arthur Conan Doyle.'

'Really?' she said again.

'Indeed.'

'Would you happen to know his address?'

'People write to him care of Baker Street and here at *The Strand*.'

'Baker Street?'

'Yes, 221B,' said the young man playfully teasing his visitor. 'Which of course you know being a devotee of Mr Holmes.'

Mrs Hudson smiled. 'I take Mr Holmes his mail, and he does receive many strange requests, but my notes are not for Mr Holmes but for publication.'

Ernest gave a weak smile. *What is she talking about?* Then he returned to the subject. 'But the best address is Sir Arthur Conan Doyle, Crowborough, East Sussex. That is sure to find him.'

He walked to the front door and held it open for the now better informed but still confused Mrs Hudson.

'Good day, madam,' he said, smiling, 'and good luck.'

Without being pushed, Mrs Hudson found herself being pushed into Burleigh Street where she pondered her next move.

She considered taking the manuscript home and forgetting about the whole blessed thing. She considered posting the manuscript to this Arthur Conan Doyle chap, whoever he might be. She considered taking the manuscript to meet the man in person.

Studying her watch, and the contents of her purse, she decided.

Chapter 6

THE TRAIN ARRIVED AT CROWBOROUGH. Mrs Hudson alighted and appeared lost. She'd never been to Sussex, East or West. The other passengers knew their destinations and vacated the platform.

The stationmaster saw the elderly woman alone and unsure. He moved to her. 'Can I assist you, madam? This is Crowborough and Jarvis Brook Station.'

'Thank you,' she said. 'I'm looking for the home of Sir Arthur Conan Doyle. Is it far?'

'Windlesham Manor is almost two miles from here, madam. I recommend you take a cab. Please come this way.' He escorted her to the gate and pointed at a man sitting on his trap.

'Oh, thank you,' she said.

'May I have your ticket please, madam?' asked the SM.

She fossicked in her basket, the one which contained her precious manuscript. Out came her ticket, the cabman accepted his passenger, and the journey to Sir Arthur's home began.

'No, no, no!' The voice sounded rich with frustration and anger. 'How many more times, Woodie? No interviews without an appointment, and under no circumstances will I see any of those fanatics.'

Sir Arthur Conan Doyle berated his long-serving friend and secretary, Major Alfred Herbert Wood. The two men first met when Doyle began practising medicine in Southsea decades ago. They became friends and shared interests playing golf, cricket and football together. They travelled to war zones in France in WW1, and so it seemed a natural move for bachelor Wood to become Doyle's secretary and right hand man.

'But Arthur, she's elderly, has come all the way from London on her own, and is desperate to see you. Surely five minutes of your valuable time, please.'

Sir Arthur heaved a super sigh. 'All right, but stress that five minutes is all I can spare.'

'I'll show her in.' Wood stopped at the door and spoke quickly. 'Her name is Mrs Hudson.'

Sir Arthur opened his mouth to shout but the secretary made a snappy exit fearing the response from his employer.

The famous writer lived a busy, sometimes hectic life feted by royalty and politicians, by leading figures in the armed forces, by fellow writers, by real policemen, and increasingly by believers in the world of spiritualism. His adoring public demanded more detective tales, and he became a favourite with members of the *Crimes Club*.

But with fame came interruptions, and many came from the fanatical fans of his hugely popular creation, Sherlock Holmes.

People wrote to Sir Arthur. The postal service worked long and hard dealing with his correspondence. People asked for help wanting the fictional detective to tackle their particular issue. People stopped Sir Arthur in the street. Some even called him Mr Holmes. Sir Arthur struggled to accept there were so many people convinced Sherlock Holmes walked the streets as a real person.

No wonder the Scottish doctor cum writer loathed the Baker Street sleuth. No wonder Sir Arthur gleefully shoved Sherlock off a ledge and into the Reichenbach Falls in Switzerland.

But the death of Holmes—fake as it turned out—did nothing to stop his popularity, and still the letters and callers came. Wood operated under strict instructions—no fanatics!

The secretary appeared. 'Your visitor, Sir Arthur; it's Mrs Hudson.' Wood departed and Sir Arthur stood, his perfect manners de rigueur. 'How do you do, madam? Please be seated.'

'Thank you, sir,' she said, and sat in the famous man's study, an impressive room in an impressive house; not ostentatious but it reeked of the success the writer achieved thanks to his detective tales.

'I don't normally see anyone without an appointment, madam, and I am very busy, so please state your business without delay.'

Mrs Hudson withdrew her manuscript and placed it on her lap.

'I have written a memoir, sir, of my life as landlady to the great detective, Sherlock Holmes, and his friend Dr Watson.'

Sir Arthur sighed in exasperation. He'd long ago lost count of the number of pastiches from budding authors who took his characters and wrote their own version of a mystery starring Holmes and Watson. Here sat yet another deluded would-be author seeking support for her, no doubt, tawdry prose.

'I regret, madam, you've had a wasted trip. I have neither the time nor interest to read the vast number of manuscripts which find their way to my home.'

'But I was told, sir, you are responsible for the cases of Sherlock Holmes being published in *The Strand Magazine*.'

'I think you'll find the editor, Mr Greenhough Smith is the person responsible.'

'I beg your pardon?'

'As everyone knows, I wrote the stories but it is the publisher who controls the content and printing of the magazine.'

Mrs Hudson gasped. Sir Arthur noted her shock and tried to explain. *She's not only a fantasist but blissfully ignorant.*

'My dear lady, authors write and publishers publish; it is the way of the world of business.'

Alarm covered the visitor's face. 'Did I hear you correctly, sir? Did you say *you* wrote the cases solved by Mr Holmes?'

Sir Arthur smiled becoming a tad patronising. 'I think the whole world is aware of such a fact, madam.'

'But surely that can't be true. I know the cases were written by Dr John H. Watson. I often heard Dr Watson and Mr Holmes discussing his writing. I've even seen handwritten pages from time to time when I cleared away their supper dishes.'

Sir Arthur winced. Here we go again. Another reader convinced Sherlock Holmes was, *is* a real person. Explaining the truth to devoted readers often proved painful for both speaker and listener. In this case it became pathetic with the deluded fan being elderly.

'I fear, madam, you are confusing the world of fiction with reality. Dr Watson trained as a medical man, as did I, but there the comparison ends. Dr John H. Watson is a figment of my imagination, and the man is as much invented as Saunders McMucklebuckle and Flora Spits.'

Mrs Hudson thought she sat before a madman. *Who is this man?* She'd been the landlady to Dr Watson for many years and, after he married and departed Baker Street, he often popped in to see his friend, Mr Holmes. Of course Dr Watson is real. She took his hat and gloves the other night. She walked up the stairs beside him. She handed him a glass for his farewell drink with Mr Holmes.

Why, even the young man she met in reception at *The Strand* told her about Sir Arthur being the literary agent who handled the stories about Sherlock Holmes, the stories written by Dr Watson. Now her former tenant's literary agent claimed *he* was the author. How scandalous. What would Dr Watson say to this outrageous claim? What would Mr Holmes do?

'I'll have you know, sir, I spoke with Dr Watson only yesterday.'

'Oh,' replied the author deciding to humour his visitor. 'And how is the dear old chap?'

'He's well but upset.'

'Nothing serious I hope.'

'Dr Watson worries that Mr Holmes is not handling his forthcoming retirement at all well.'

'Ah, Mr Sherlock Holmes; and you say he is retiring?'

'He's soon to leave Baker Street and become an apiarist on the Sussex Downs.'

Sir Arthur lied. 'Well as I'm here in East Sussex, perhaps Mr Holmes might care to pop in for tea. Please give him my kind regards.'

Mrs Hudson stored that information and indicated her manuscript. 'And I have promised not to publish my memoir about being the landlady to Mr Holmes and Dr Watson until both have left their home in Baker Street.'

'Ah, so you are *the* Mrs Hudson,' smiled Sir Arthur, still managing to grind his teeth. 'If only you had said so before.'

Finally the visitor thought progress was being made. She placed her manuscript on his desk and stated her request.

'I would be most grateful, sir, if you could act as *my* literary agent, and take this memoir to *The Strand Magazine*.'

Sir Arthur stared at the face of his sincere but deluded visitor. He decided. This farce must end. He stood.

'Alas I am unable to assist, madam.' Mrs Hudson frowned.

'Please, sir,' she begged. 'I have found many mistakes in Dr Watson's tales and reveal all such errors in my memoir.'

'Mistakes?' said Sir Arthur as his dander popped up and glared.

'Poor Dr Watson rushed to finish a number of cases and often got details jumbled. He would write nothing for ages and then hurry to complete several in record time as *The Strand Magazine* pushed him for more of the cases solved by Mr Holmes; hence the mistakes.'

Sir Arthur scowled. *How does she know that? It's true of course but who told her? This woman is not the usual fanatic.*

He'd met many devoted fans over the years but never one like this woman; someone with the temerity to point out mistakes in his writing, and furthermore to tell the truth about his rushed production schedule of new Sherlockian stories. He didn't seethe but any more such comments and watch out Mrs H.

'Unfortunately madam, I, like Sherlock Holmes, have retired. My days are now spent investigating real crimes, and in travelling the world to tell mankind about the power and benefits of spiritualism.' He handed Mrs Hudson her manuscript. 'Good day to you, Mrs Hudson.'

She appeared ready to cry. Her dream, her years of work, her hopes were dashed. Major Wood, hovering in the corridor, appeared and took her arm.

'Come along, Mrs Hudson. Let's leave Sir Arthur to get on with his important work.' He led her from the study.

'But sir,' she whispered as Sir Arthur returned to his book on spiritualism.

'This way, madam,' said the secretary, and escorted Mrs Hudson to the front door. He sensed her disappointment.

She muttered. 'Sir Arthur did a brilliant job as literary agent for Dr Watson. How I wish he could do the same for me, and my manuscript reveals so much about Mr Holmes.'

'Have you thought about approaching the editor of *The Strand Magazine* yourself?' asked Major Wood.

Mrs Hudson stood still. Her disappointment faded as this new idea took hold. She beamed. 'Oh, do you think I could?'

'Indeed. Nothing ventured, nothing gained, Mrs Hudson. The gentleman's name is Mr Herbert Greenough Smith.'

He opened the door for the landlady from London. She smiled, thanked Woodie, and set off down the path with a renewed spring in her step. She climbed into the waiting cab for the trip back to Crowborough where she again caught the train operated by the London, Brighton and South Coast Railway.

Chapter 7

MRS HUDSON ARRIVED AT LONDON BRIDGE, one of the oldest railway stations in the world, and hailed a cab. She alighted in Burleigh Street where, with her manuscript, she once again entered the office of *The Strand Magazine*.

'Good afternoon, madam,' said Ernest, the same young man she met earlier. 'Have you posted your manuscript to Sir Arthur?'

She produced it. 'No, I showed it to him in person.'

'My goodness, you are brave,' said the surprised young man.

'And his secretary, Mr Woodie, recommended I show it to the editor, Mr Herbert Greenhough Smith.'

Shock appeared on Ernest's face. 'Sir Arthur read your manuscript?' Mrs Hudson chose a smile for her answer. 'And Major Wood suggested you show it to Mr Greenhough Smith?'

Mrs Hudson's smile grew larger.

'Now young man, I don't have an appointment but as Sir Arthur and his secretary were so supportive, could you please ask if Mr Greenhough Smith might see me? I can explain my book in a few minutes.'

Mrs Hudson used the magic phrase, Sir Arthur. At *The Strand*, mention of Sir Arthur's name became a synonym for *Open sesame*.

'I'll speak with the editor. And I'm afraid I've forgotten your name.'

She straightened. 'Mrs Hudson, landlady to Mr Sherlock Holmes.'

The young man indicated a chair. 'Please take a seat, Mrs Hudson.'

He left and she heard muffled voices coming from elsewhere in the building. There seemed to be some sort of argument. The voices fell silent and the assistant re-appeared.

'Please come this way, Mrs Hudson.'

They approached an office with the word *Editor* on the door. The assistant knocked and Mrs Hudson met Mr Herbert Greenhough Smith, editor of *The Strand Magazine*, the man who published almost all of Sir Arthur's stories about the internationally famous Sherlock Holmes, the detective who lived in Baker Street with a landlady who now, apparently, stood in the said editor's London office. She knew her identity. He didn't have a clue.

'I believe you were referred to us by Major Wood,' said Herbert indicating a chair for his visitor. They both sat.

'I was, sir, and am delighted to meet you,' replied Mrs Hudson.

'How may I help?'

Now on a roll, and indicating her manuscript, she let fly. 'I have written a memoir of my life as landlady to Mr Sherlock Holmes and Dr John H. Watson.'

Herbert's eyes widened. Over the years he'd received countless approaches from budding authors but this one seemed unusual.

'So you are a student of the great detective's cases?' he asked.

'Naturally I've read all of Dr Watson's stories, sir, but my memoir is written from a unique perspective.'

The editor's heart beat quicker. 'And in what way is it unique?'

'Surely you must know the answer.' His face remained blank. She couldn't believe his tardy response and ignorance. 'Why, sir, I'm actually *in* the cases. You must have seen my name.'

Disappointment slapped the editor. *Oh dear. Here sits one of those disillusioned and pathetic readers Sir Arthur tells me about.*

He played a straight bat. 'Mrs Hudson, you say?'

'Indeed, Mrs Hudson, the landlady of Mr Holmes and Dr Watson, although the good doctor has since married, more than once I believe, and moved to live with his good ladies, er, lady.'

Now while Sir Arthur and Major Wood encountered many Sherlockian crackpots, Greenhough Smith used staff, at times known as gatekeepers, to shield him from such interlopers. This time however they failed. Herbert faced a full-blown fanatic.

Has this quaint, septuagenarian escaped from an institution?

'I see,' replied the editor. 'And you say you've written a memoir?'

'Nobody had the intimate relationship I shared with Mr Holmes and Dr Watson. I had a unique, fly-on-the-wall perspective of those gentlemen as they interviewed would-be clients from criminals to kings.'

Mrs Hudson skipped into action. This lively aspect of her personality had, until last night, remained hidden. In his writing, Dr Watson failed abysmally to notice the landlady's strengths. And the best the great observer Sherlock Holmes came up with was, "She has as good an idea of breakfast as a Scotchwoman".

She spoke in hushed tones. 'And what's more, sir, I have notated the many mistakes made by Dr Watson.'

'Mistakes?' asked the editor.

'Not to mention the failures of Mr Holmes himself.'

Herbert didn't know how to react, which meant trouble for him because worse loomed large.

'I'm surprised you, as their editor, failed to correct these blunders, many of them elementary.'

Herbert reacted as did Holmes when Mrs Hudson first dropped her bombshell. The editor spluttered while his guest continued her attack.

'I understand *The Strand* has done very well out of Dr Watson's writing, but surely editorial standards must be maintained. Has the publishing world decided that "close enough is good enough"? Do you not conduct basic research of so-called facts to ensure their accuracy?'

Once the initial shock drained from Herbert's body, he joined the conversation on a more even footing.

'Now you say Major Wood referred ...'

'Woodie,' she corrected the editor. 'I heard Sir Arthur refer to his secretary as Woodie.'

Herbert nodded. 'Of course, so Major Woodie referred you to me.'

'He did. His exact words were, "The gentleman's name is Mr Herbert Greenough Smith".'

'And does Sir Arthur know of your manuscript?'

'He most certainly does. I interviewed the gentleman only this morning but regret to say he proved to be useless.'

The editor's eyebrows climbed. Describing his most popular writer as "useless" shocked. 'Did you say useless, madam?'

Mrs Hudson sat tall then spoke with serious intent. 'I can't be sure of my opinion, but I fear the man suffers from delusions of grandeur.'

The editor had no idea where this conversation was heading.

'Sir Arthur is deluded? In what way, may I ask?'

'He made the astonishing claim that *he* wrote the cases solved by Mr Holmes.'

'I see,' replied the editor, convinced the woman had escaped from a secure unit. He wondered if she carried any type of weapon; after all the suffragettes used violence proving it was not the sole prerogative of the male sex. Herbert began planning to remove this convincing but totally deluded woman. But she sat still and strong, not going anywhere, and continued.

'The most shocking thing I heard from Sir Arthur involved his claim about Dr Watson being an imaginary figure. Can I remember his words? Ah yes, Dr Watson is "a figment of my imagination".'

'And you dispute that of course?'

Mrs Hudson gave Herbert a weary look.

What is wrong with these men? Here sits the second person today to treat me like a simpleton. What sort of a question is that?

Dr Watson, the man she first met decades ago, who lived under her roof for years, and who still called to see his friend Sherlock Holmes is what, a ghost, a walking, talking apparition?

'I assure you sir I have all my faculties which are in sound working order. I have the usual ailments of a woman my age, certainly my limbs are arthritic, but my brain is absolutely first-class.'

'Forgive me, Mrs Hudson, I did not wish to cause offence.'

'I must admit, sir, I'm disappointed at your lack of enthusiasm towards my manuscript. I can understand Mr Holmes and Sir Arthur's lack of interest—both have a lot to lose—but you, sir, you could capitalize on the popularity of Dr Watson's tales and use my memoir to make a king's ransom.' The woman's logic joined her superb delivery and built the intrigue.

'You say you showed your manuscript to Sherlock Holmes?'

'I pointed out misleading claims and blatant errors, and he passed them off as if they didn't exist.'

'And when did this happen? Your meeting with Mr Holmes I mean?'

'Last night.' She paused. 'Or was it the night before?' Herbert knew she was bonkers. 'He's retiring and moving to the country.'

'I see. And Sir Arthur told you this?'

Mrs Hudson's frustration increased.

Why can't this so-called editor understand my simple statements?

'No, Mr *Holmes* told me, and I could hardly fail to notice. The sitting-room is awash with his packing, but until he actually leaves, I refuse to allow my manuscript to be published. That is most important.'

She assumed it would be published, snapped up because the authoress had spent decades caring for Mr Holmes and Dr Watson.

The more Mrs Hudson prattled on, the more fascinating she became to Greenhough Smith. His urge to send her away was tempered by his admiration for her stunning performance. *Is she a professional actress? I've never seen her on the stage.* He knew she could definitely be certified but her ability to appear genuine hooked him. *I've heard it said narcissists can hide in plain sight.*

'May I ask why you choose to delay your memoir's publication?'

'I've already told you, sir. It would be the height of bad manners to reveal the faults, faux pas and foibles of my tenants while the gentlemen are still in the public eye.'

'I see. That's highly commendable.'

'However, I could never disappoint the vast number of devoted followers of the famous sleuth and his friend, all of whom would be shocked to know that in real life, Mr Holmes is Mr Messy, and Dr Watson Dr Duffer.'

'Did you say "in real life"?'

More confusion showed on the face of Mrs Hudson. 'Yes. What other life is there?' He tried to explain but couldn't because she continued. 'Oh, I understand. You mean the fictional world of some of the other stories in your magazine.'

He nodded. 'Precisely.'

She moved in for the kill using, in selling terms, what would become known as the assumptive close. 'Come, sir, the world will soon be shattered to learn Mr Holmes has retired. My memoir will help fill the void.' She held up her manuscript. 'This is the true and inside story of the world's greatest consulting detective.' Interpretation: You know you want it, Herbie.

Herbert's fascination ended when his common sense prevailed. Today his world was ruled by editorial decisions and printing deadlines. To spend time with a woman, clearly 'away with the fairies', would not get his magazine published. He stood.

'Madam, you must excuse me. I do have a hectic schedule.'

She stood, believing he spoke the truth but certain he regarded her as credible and her writing as the best thing since Sherlock Holmes.

'I'll leave my memoir in your capable hands, sir. But please respect my wishes and publish nothing until I advise you that Mr Holmes has well and truly retired.'

Herbert wanted to send the woman packing together with her manuscript but realised the quickest and easiest way to be rid of her would be to acquiesce. He escorted her to the front office.

'Thank you, kindly Mrs Hudson. I shall be in touch.'

He nodded to his assistant and retired to his office. Mrs Hudson felt no need to leave and began chatting to Ernest. He needed instructions from the boss.

Is this woman a contributor to The Strand? Should I take her details?

To be safe he did. Finally, he opened the door and bade farewell to the eccentric old biddy from Baker Street.

Five minutes later, the editor burst in distraught.

'Where is she?' cried Herbert. 'That woman, Mrs Hudson, where is she?'

'She's gone, Mr Greenhough Smith.'

He despaired. 'Gone! Gone where?'

'I have no idea, sir,' said the now despairing junior.

'Well go and fetch her.'

'Sir?'

'Bring her back man, don't let her escape. Go!'

Ernest fled leaving Herbert pacing the reception area, hoping and praying his potential bestselling author would return.

After Mrs Hudson left his office, out of curiosity, he picked up the crackpot's manuscript to see what a fanatic might write. Great Lord of Mercy! The contents gripped him. He discovered gold. The woman's imagination blossomed like nothing he'd ever seen. It put Conan Doyle's prose in the shade. If the cases of Sherlock Holmes were popular, this exposé of the private lives and writing errors of Holmes and Watson was, for the publisher, manna from Heaven.

Herbert often wondered when the income from Sir Arthur's pen would start to wane. With Mrs Hudson's memoir, Sherlock's stories could boom again. This manuscript would not only appeal to the fans of Holmes, it would create a new and much wider audience. The hoi polloi craved intimate details of famous people like Holmes and Watson, and here they were in stunning detail. Mrs Hudson's memoir screamed publisher's goldmine. *Where is that boy?*

Ernest burst into the reception area panting.

'Where is she?' demanded the editor.

'I'm sorry, Mr Greenhough Smith, she's gone.'

'Gone! She can't have gone, she's a hundred years old. For God's sake, man, she's got rheumatoid arthritis!'

'She must have hailed a cab, sir.'

'But I need to find her. Her manuscript is the best I've ever seen.'

'I do have her address, Mr Greenhough Smith.'

The editor changed in an instant. His fury and despair became relief and delight.

'Thank goodness, stout fellow. Well, tell me, tell me,' he urged.

Ernest produced a notepad and read. 'Ah Mrs Hudson ... she didn't give her first name.'

'Never mind that. What's her address?'

Ernest read what he'd written. 'It's ... 221B Baker Street, London.'

The editor exploded. 'You blithering idiot!'

The assistant stammered in confusion. 'But isn't that the address of Mr Sherlock Holmes?'

If looks could kill, Ernest was already reclining in a funeral parlour.

The editor bellowed. 'There's no such address. It's fictional, made up, invented by Sir Arthur! Baker Street is short and only goes up to about number 100.'

In the hope of saving his career, even his skin, Ernest threw what would become known as a Hail Mary pass. Losing badly, he needed a result and quickly, so to change his fortunes, he played what he hoped would be a blinder of an idea. 'Perhaps Sir Arthur might know,' he squeaked.

Fortunately the editor ignored him. 'What am I going to do?' asked the desperate Greenhough Smith. 'I've found an author with the perfect manuscript and I don't know where she lives. I don't even know her first name.'

Ernest thought about suggesting Sherlock Holmes might know but decided against that idea. The assistant couldn't bring himself to look at his employer who stormed out of Reception.

'Damn, damn and double damn,' he roared.

Chapter 8

AS MRS HUDSON TRAVELLED BY TRAIN to and from Sussex, Holmes and Watson conducted a serious and in-depth analysis of her manuscript. They both worried.

Watson's meeting with Holmes last night proved an eye-opener. For Watson it was a toss-up as to which event was the more shocking—Mrs Hudson's writing expertise and the content of her memoir, or the major personality change displayed by his friend.

'What has she done with her manuscript?' asked Watson.

Sherlock snapped. 'I have no idea. It's gone, and so is she without a by your leave or so much as a "Good day Mr Holmes".'

Watson tried to calm his friend. 'I seem to remember Mrs Hudson would often tell us where she was going.'

'She's taken the manuscript to your literary agent,' replied Holmes.

'What? Are you sure? Did she say that?'

'Eliminate all other factors, and the one which remains must be the truth. If you don't know my methods by now, Watson, you never will.'

Both men were at a loss. They knew the contents of Mrs Hudson's memoir were dynamite. They survived the initial shock period, and now endured the worry period. The thought of their mistakes, blunders and personal habits being recorded brought stress. The thought of such detail being published in the organ which brought their triumphs to the attention of readers around the globe, caused both men acute discomfort.

'Tell me about this literary agent of yours,' said Holmes.

'As I said, he's a medical man turned writer who supplements his meagre income representing honest scribblers like myself.'

'What sort of a name is Conan Doyle?'

'I think he uses one of his given names to make a sort of double-barrelled surname.'

'Affectatious,' snorted Holmes.

Watson feared he might further upset his friend. 'Possibly. But the editor at *The Strand* has done the same thing.' Holmes appeared puzzled. 'Herbert Smith calls himself Herbert Greenhough Smith.'

'Snobbery,' said Holmes. 'I can't imagine you calling yourself Hamish Watson.'

Watson struggled. 'Why on Earth would I do that?'

'I don't know. Perhaps you lack self-confidence or wish to inflate your sense of self-importance.'

'I don't follow any of that but why would I use Hamish?'

Holmes stared at his friend. 'Dr John H. Watson.'

'But the H doesn't stand for Hamish.'

'Well Harry, Horace or Hannibal—you take my point.'

Watson sounded short. 'No, I don't.'

They fell silent. Of good news came there none. This unique manuscript had rattled Holmes good and proper. Watson wasn't all that solid either.

'Can this chap be trusted?' asked Holmes.

'Who, Greenough Smith?'

'No, Conan Doyle.'

'I haven't contacted him for ages; certainly not since your Swiss holiday.'

'Can you ask him to hold on to the manuscript until we decide how to deal with it?'

'But we don't know what Mrs Hudson has done with it. And besides, it has nothing to do with us.'

'My dear Watson,' argued Holmes, now agitated. 'It has *every*thing to do with us. We are its raison d'etre.'

'But we had nothing to do with its creation.'

'Oh please, Watson, this is no time to split hairs. The memoir damns us both. My legacy is in danger of being tarnished forever, and yours too, although yours was never well polished in the first place.'

Watson recoiled. He knew his friend battled extreme pressure. His imminent retirement brought on his depression, and now this exposé of his errors and private life only added to his melancholy. But really, Holmes had overstepped the line with such an unkind remark.

'I rarely see the fellow, Holmes. He's gone a bit strange in recent years taking an interest in spiritualism.'

Holmes scoffed. 'There are no ghosts in this world. Save those we make for ourselves.'

Watson sought a peaceful solution. "I'm sure we can appeal to Mrs Hudson's kind nature.'

Holmes scoffed. '*You* may appeal, Watson; but she'll never listen to me.' Watson despaired at Holmes' negativity. 'I've been ordering the woman from this room for decades.' He imitated himself. 'Thank you, Mrs Hudson. That will do, Mrs Hudson. That is all, Mrs Hudson.'

'And she followed your every request without hesitation.'

'But rarely willingly. I tell you, Watson, she hates me.'

Watson's eyes opened wide. He reckoned Holmes had now as good as impugned the honour of a lady. 'Now see here, Holmes; that is an outrageous thing to say.'

'She's getting back at me for treating her like a servant. I'm sure I've shouted at the woman on many occasions.'

Watson boiled. 'Holmes; you are completely wrong. There were countless times when Mrs Hudson told me how much she admired and worried about you.'

Holmes stopped. 'Mrs Hudson admired and worried about me?'

Watson nodded. Holmes fell silent. He pondered the situation.

Am I overreacting? I failed to spot her intelligence and wit, and obvious writing skills. Maybe I should have asked her to document my cases and leave Watson to get on with finding his wives.

The afternoon drifted into evening. Both men worried although for different reasons. The clock chimed but it was the sound of the front door being opened that grabbed their attention.

'It's her, she's back,' said Holmes. 'Ask her to come in.'

'*You* must ask her, Holmes. You're the tenant, I'm the visitor.'

Holmes glared at Watson, strode to the door and called. 'Mrs Hudson. Would you be so kind as to favour us with your presence?'

Silence. The already tense atmosphere ratcheted even higher.

Her voice was heard from afar. 'Coming, Mr Holmes.'

Both men stood waiting for Mrs Hudson's entrance. Good old Mrs Hudson, the ever quiet, loyal, reliable, wouldn't-say-boo-to-a-goose landlady. Her soft footsteps sounded loud. Holmes surveyed the mess he'd made with his still unfinished packing. Watson surveyed Holmes.

'Be kind, Holmes,' he whispered as Mrs Hudson entered the room.

'Good evening, gentlemen,' she said.

'Good evening, Mrs Hudson,' they replied in unison.

'I do apologise, Mr Holmes, but urgent business took me away from Baker Street today. But I'm returned as you see and I'll attend to your supper. Will you be joining us, Dr Watson?'

The men spoke simultaneously. Holmes wanted to say supper meant nothing to him, and Watson tried to tell her he would not be staying. They were embarrassed at their overlapping babble.

'I think I understood,' she replied, and turned to leave. She knew the topic and tone of discussion to follow and wanted no part of it.

'Mrs Hudson,' requested the detective, 'please be so kind as to take a seat.' She paused then acquiesced. The males remained standing.

'Before you begin, Mr Holmes, I wish to say something.' Even now Holmes did not have the first word. Again she beat him to the punch. 'Over the years I have learnt so much from you, sir, with one of the main lessons being a gentleman's word is his bond.' She paused, milking the situation. It was no understatement to say the landlady controlled the meeting. She continued.

'Please be assured gentlemen, when I said I would never publish a word of my memoir unless and until both of you are safely ensconced in your retirement and well away from the prying eyes of the public, I meant it. I too believe a lady's word is her bond.'

Watson was thrilled. Holmes breathed a tad easier and replied.

'That is most kind of you, Mrs Hudson. I would have expected nothing less from a woman of such rectitude and outstanding character.'

Holmes meant every word of his reply but Watson wondered if his friend had any choice in the matter.

Still, the doctor gaped in awe. This type of conversation between these two people had never been heard before. Watson's hopes edged higher. *This*, he thought, *may yet end well.*

But as so often before, Watson's hopes were hopelessly wrong.

The trio tippy-toed around the subject of the day—more like of the century—with no-one wanting to say something they would later regret. Mrs Hudson was still on a high following her travels and conversations. Watson desperately wanted peace and to maintain the relationship between the tenants and their landlady, or in his case, former landlady. Holmes wanted to know precisely the entire content of her manuscript and what she planned to do with it.

'I've been busy, gentlemen,' said Mrs Hudson. 'Two trips to *The Strand Magazine*, and one to the countryside in glorious Sussex.'

Her statement shocked both men who had questions galore.

'How interesting,' said Holmes keeping his bombastic behaviour in check—just. 'I can understand the need to visit the magazine but am curious as to your trip to the countryside, madam.'

She wanted to explain her success, and with her famous tenant being abnormally subdued and unusually polite, she spoke with enthusiasm giving full details.

'The editor of *The Strand Magazine* proved to be most helpful,' she said and Watson's mouth opened involuntarily. 'Mr Greenhough Smith kindly afforded me an interview being most impressed with my work and references.'

The fact the elderly landlady travelled alone to London and Sussex was impressive in itself. To have met with at least one important person in the publishing world made her actions remarkable.

'You had an appointment with the editor, Mr Greenhough Smith?' asked Watson.

'Indeed and my manuscript made a great impression, so much so he retained it to prepare its publication.'

Like many budding authors, Mrs Hudson acquired the art of exaggeration, white lie telling and bald face lying. Holmes felt his skills of Bartitsu and boxing were long gone as Mrs Hudson landed a telling blow to his empty bread basket, now literally empty because she couldn't arrange meals being out and about arranging her publishing contract. Talk about a double whammy.

'Greenhough Smith has your manuscript with a view to publishing it?' asked Watson, looking like a prisoner awaiting execution.

She smiled and nodded and Holmes, seriously worried, asked, 'And your trip to Sussex, Mrs Hudson; may one ask its purpose?'

'I went to interview Dr Watson's literary agent, a doctor, Sir Arthur Conan Doyle.' The men exchanged glances. 'I must say he proved difficult and I suspect the man is either a criminal, a lunatic or both.'

The claims and comments from the humble landlady continued in quantity and quality. They were outlandish but were they true?

'You make some remarkable claims, Mrs Hudson,' said Holmes. Her comments seemed normal to her.

'Did you say Sir Arthur Conan Doyle is a criminal?' asked an incredulous Watson. 'Or that he's *insane?*'

She leant forward and spoke in a soft voice; unnecessary because no-one outside the room could have heard even if she shouted. Her acting skills were on show. Instinctively, Holmes and Watson made involuntary reciprocal moves forward in order to hear.

'The man confessed to being the author of Dr Watson's tales as published in *The Strand Magazine.*'

'He what?' snapped Watson, feeling bile rise in his mouth.

'Naturally I told him you, Dr Watson, are the author, and I had even seen your written manuscripts at different times when clearing away the supper dishes.'

'Thank you, Mrs Hudson,' said Watson feeling even more admiration for his favourite landlady.

'And how did this literary agent take your news?' asked Holmes.

'To be honest, gentlemen, he responded abruptly and with rudeness. I got the distinct feeling he considered me a simpleton and worse, a liar.' Holmes, and especially Watson, flared. 'He refused to consider my manuscript or act as my literary agent as he does for you, Dr Watson.'

'I apologise for his ungentlemanly behaviour, Mrs Hudson,' said Watson, 'and certainly for his foolishness in rejecting your admirable prose.' She smiled at the good doctor. Even if he wanted to, Holmes couldn't smile.

'Then how, dear lady,' asked the detective, 'were you able to obtain an appointment with Mr Greenhough Smith?'

'Ah, Sir Arthur's secretary, Major Woodie, encouraged me to call again at *The Strand*. I did and told them I'd been to see Sir Arthur Conan Doyle and that seemed to impress them and so,' she opened her palms, 'in I went, here I am and, as they say, the rest is history.'

Silence spoke next. It bubbled. Different emotions were in play.

For Mrs Hudson, to have travelled all that way and persevered lifted her spirits. To have left her manuscript with a leading editor gave her happiness quotient a serious boost.

Alas, not so her companions. Watson, as per usual, could be described as either mildly pleased or mildly distressed. On the quiet, Holmes fumed.

In Sussex, the so-called fraudster, Sir Arthur, dressed for his excursion. His attire and footwear were important with his destination London for an activity with fellow members of the *Crimes Club*. After dark, the crime-loving gents were to tour Jack the Ripper sites in London's East End.

'Damn tie,' muttered Sir Arthur, fiddling.

Wood coughed outside Sir Arthur's room. 'Excuse me, Arthur.'

'Come in, Woodie. Tell me, what does one wear to go creeping around dark alleys in Whitechapel and Spitalfields? How do I look?'

'I doubt there'll be a competition for the best-dressed amateur detective, Arthur.'

Miffed, Sir Arthur dismissed his secretary. 'I thought you'd left.'

'I stopped because this telegram arrived. It's from Greenhough Smith.'

Fixing his tie, Sir Arthur reckoned he looked ready for the Ripper tour. 'What does he want? I told him no more Holmes, not for all the tea in China.' More tie fiddling. 'Well go on, read the jolly thing.'

Wood felt queasy as he read aloud.

'*Dear Sir Arthur. A thousand thanks for the Mrs Hudson referral. Her manuscript is magnificent. Letter following. Yours etc, Herbert Greenough Smith.*'

Sir Arthur genuinely misunderstood. 'What's he talking about, a Mrs Hudson referral?'

Wood happily referred Mrs Hudson to Greenhough Smith believing she would be sent packing. Not so. To Wood's alarm, the editor seems to have welcomed the little old lady; actually, more than welcomed.

'I think he's referring to the little old lady who called earlier today with her memoir of life in Baker Street. Apparently she paid a visit to the magazine in London.'

Wood's belief that trouble would soon begin to brew proved correct when Sir Arthur let loose. 'But she's delusional, not right in the head, and I gave her no such referral.'

'Ah,' said Wood looking sheepish. 'That may be my fault.'

Sir Arthur bristled. 'Woodie, what have you done?'

'I sent her to *The Strand* to get her out of your hair, Arthur.'

The knight groaned. 'Oh Woodie; how many times? Do not give deluded fanatics and self-published scribblers any encouragement.'

'Yes, Arthur. But at least she's out of your life for good.'

Doyle growled. 'For your sake, I hope so. Now, if you please, kindly help me find my cap and stick.'

Chapter 9

SIR ARTHUR CAME DOWN from London late that night. Having a motorcar made life much more convenient. The tour of Jack the Ripper sites with fellow members of the *Crimes Club* went well. Sir Arthur chose not to mention he made a similar trip years ago, during Queen Victoria's reign. Sherlock Holmes had surged in the popularity stakes, and as Scotland Yard made zero progress in cracking the case, they were willing to try anything to catch the Ripper. Why not ask a successful crime fiction writer? He might see something they failed to spot. Some hope. More like no hope.

All those years ago when news of Dr Doyle's first Whitechapel excursion reached Baker Street, Sherlock Holmes scoffed and Dr Watson chose not to mention Conan Doyle acted as his literary agent. Mrs Hudson heard part of the discussion and duly inscribed her scrapbook but knew nothing of a certain literary agent at the time.

Next morning, in his study, Sir Arthur worked on his latest speech. A group of spiritualists invited him to address their group and he wanted to make his lecture as effective as possible. His interest in the "other side" started decades ago but now, far more people began to discover his passion for the spirit world.

Major Wood brought in the mail. The secretary spotted a letter from Greenhough Smith, and following yesterday's London telegram, expected this missive. He worried, dreading the contents.

'The mail, Arthur, including something from Greenhough Smith.'

Sir Arthur groaned. 'No, he's wasting his time.'

Wood wanted out. 'I'll let you get on.'

Sir Arthur glared at his secretary. Words were not required. The unhappy doctor's eyes warned Major Wood of the forthcoming volley.

'Stay, Woodie. I want you to hear this.' Sir Arthur opened the letter. 'This is all your fault. Why on Earth did you send the deluded old biddy to *The Strand?*' Sir Arthur glanced at the letter.

'I took pity on her, Arthur. She's elderly, came all the way from London, and I thought Greenhough Smith would send her away with a flea in her ear.'

'Hardly; Greenhough Smith thinks she's written a masterpiece.'

'What! Really? Are you joking?' gasped Wood.

He wasn't. 'And she didn't tell you her real name?'

'Just Mrs Hudson.'

Sir Arthur read aloud.

> *Dear Sir Arthur*
> *I wish to thank you for sending the elderly lady calling herself Mrs Hudson. As you no doubt saw, her manuscript is truly remarkable. Her understanding of your famous characters is so accurate I felt I was reading your prose.*

Doyle shook his head and glared at his secretary. 'How many times have I warned you about these fanatics?'

'I'm sorry, Arthur. I thought if ...'

'You're not paid to think, Woodie, but to protect me from these people, who, for some inexplicable reason, believe Mr Sherlock Bloody Holmes is a real person.' Wood breathed a little easier but not for long. Sir Arthur resumed reading aloud.

> *However, when she explained how she discovered so many basic mistakes in your text, I studied the memoir in detail and was shocked to see her statement is true. I admit to a deep sense of shame. My editorial skills failed and did so abysmally. Please accept my sincere apologies for such an oversight.*

Doyle looked at the intimidated Wood then re-read a part of the letter. 'And what does "*so many basic mistakes in your text*" mean?'

Wood struggled. 'It can't be true, Arthur. You yourself said the woman is delusional.'

Sir Arthur fumed then read the next two lines to himself. 'Oh, this is absurd.'

'Arthur?'

The author continued to read aloud, the tone of his voice becoming more pained as each sentence unfolded. Wood cringed.

> *I am anxious to publish Mrs Hudson's wonderful manuscript and wondered if you might assist to that end. Would you be kind enough to write a foreword to her book? Do you, sir, by any chance, have the dear woman's address, and finally, do you know her real name as Mrs Hudson is clearly a pseudonym.*
> *I look forward to your reply.*
> *Yours faithfully*
> *Herbert Greenhough Smith*

Wood didn't know where to look. Sir Arthur turned bright red and exploded. 'Write a foreword to her book! What book? Do you know her real name?' He tossed the letter on his desk. 'What is this; some sort of practical joke?'

'I'm sure there's a simple explanation, Arthur.'

'Yes, Greenhough Smith has lost his mind. We met the woman. We know she's mad. She believes Holmes and Watson are real people.'

'Well she would, Arthur?'

'Would what?'

'Believe they're real people.'

Confusion reigned. 'What are you talking about, man?'

'She believes she's the real Mrs Hudson, their landlady.'

Sir Arthur placed his elbows on his desk and buried his face in his hands. The money he made from writing detective stories brought him significant wealth enabling him to indulge his passion for historical novels and spiritualism. But it all came at a price. His sanity and patience were sorely tested by thousands of devoted followers, including one elderly female crackpot calling herself Mrs Hudson.

Wood wanted to help his employer escape his depression. 'What would you like me to do, Arthur?'

He snapped. 'For the last time, Major, I would like you to stop encouraging anyone who claims Holmes and Watson are real people living in Baker Street and solving fictitious mysteries.' His voice contained a hard edge. 'Do I make myself clear?'

'Perfectly.'

'I cannot believe Greenhough Smith wants me to write a foreword to a book written by an ageing fanatic?'

'I'm not sure her age is of any importance, Arthur.'

The author's fury soared. Now he faced an accusation of ageism. 'I don't care if she's Methuselah's mistress, the woman is clearly out of her mind and yet the supposedly intelligent editor of *The Strand* has swallowed her syntax and wants me to back his preposterous plan to publish her nonsense.'

Wood wanted to end this. 'Would you like to reply, Arthur?'

'No, I would not *like* to reply; I *have* to. Take the following.' Wood took dictation. 'Dear Mr Greenhough Smith. Thank you for yours of today. Kindly understand I will under no circumstances give any backing to your client's ineffable twaddle.' Wood sneaked a peak at Sir Arthur. The doctor looked furious. He continued.

'And I find your remark about many mistakes in my manuscripts to be a poor attempt at humour.' He paused. 'Make that particularly poor. I require no further correspondence on this matter. Yours faithfully, et cetera.' He waited for Wood to finish writing. 'And I want it sent this afternoon.'

'Of course, Arthur,' said Wood who left feeling sure he dodged a bullet. Little did he know there were still five more in the chamber.

'Wait!' called Sir Arthur. Wood returned.

'Arthur?'

'Don't send it by post. Send it by telegram.'

Wood hesitated. 'Are you sure, Arthur? It's rather large.' His employer's face answered the question. 'I'll send it now.'

When Sir Arthur's telegram arrived at *The Strand*, its editor despaired. He'd been given a manuscript he knew, not thought, *knew* was a guaranteed bestseller. It would do extremely well by itself but had the potential to drive vast numbers of new readers to the adventures of Sherlock Holmes. That was the good news.

The bad news was that Greenhough Smith, having met the writer face to face, didn't collect her surname or address. He couldn't contact her. She disappeared and nobody knew where.

But not to worry because Mrs Hudson met Sir Arthur and hopefully he would know her name and address and, better still, agree to give her book a fantastic boost by writing a foreword. Or would he?

No, he wouldn't. Sir Arthur refused to give any support to a book whose contents he described as ineffable twaddle. *Twaddle!? Oh dear* thought the editor.

Did Sir Arthur actually read the manuscript? Did Mrs Hudson point out even some of the many errors in his writing? How can I find Mrs Hudson and publish her work? Will Sir Arthur's opposition ruin everything?

He summoned the publisher's best typist, Miss Roberts, and his assistant Ernest Balfour. 'Sit Miss Roberts, and type as Ernest reads.'

The editor gave Mrs Hudson's manuscript to Ernest who did as instructed allowing Miss Roberts to type the first and only copy of Mrs Hudson's riveting memoir.

There must be a copy. Herbert would not sleep if anything happened to this money-making manuscript. And no way would he give up on his search for the lady or from persuading Sir Arthur Conan Doyle to back the project.

Well Herbert, good luck with both those aims.

Chapter 10

THE EDITOR GROANED. His headache set new records for intensity and longevity. He believed Mrs Hudson had written a brilliant book revealing a catalogue of mistakes in the stories about Sherlock Holmes, and providing a fascinating insight into the private lives of Holmes and Watson. Herbert knew the book would sell like hot cakes.

But his throbbing headache continued apace due to massive problems. Mrs Hudson could not be contacted, and Sir Arthur Conan Doyle's telegram described the manuscript as laughable. She was missing and he was hissing. Sir Arthur wanted nothing to do with the book. *Damn.*

Over many years, with Sir Arthur determined to have Mr Holmes retire, Herbert tried subtle, and some not so subtle ways to encourage the famous author to keep producing Sherlockian tales. More money was the usual tactic. Every request turned into a teeth-pulling exercise. One day, the requests would be spurned for good. Now, with this stunning manuscript by an unknown author, Sir Arthur might want to fight back against the criticism of his work. Hardly—look at his latest letter.

Only one course of action remained for the editor; visit Sir Arthur in person. Do not request an interview as it would surely be refused. Call unannounced. And soon. Time became critical. Mrs Hudson could never be called a spring chicken. What if she died or became demented or lost heart and went to ground? Those thoughts filled the editor with even more distress.

Without delay, Herbert took the next train from London. He'd been to Sir Arthur's home before but couldn't escape two feelings of dread. With no appointment, he risked Sir Arthur not being at home or worse, far worse, the author being at home yet refusing to see him. However, the possible benefits were too great.

I must confront Sir Arthur.

The trap dropped him a hundred yards from the house. Herbert wanted to give as little warning of his approach as possible. It felt a bit cloak and daggerish. It was. Sir Arthur would assign this type of behavior to Holmes or one of his many adversaries.

The editor opened the gate and walked as quietly as possible to the front door. He knew Major Wood and Lady Conan Doyle were decent folk and would certainly be courteous. *But will they be helpful?*

The knock on the door sounded faint. Herbert trembled, his nerves making his door knocking apologetic. He pondered a louder knock. As he prepared to knock again, he heard a voice from the garden. With a distinctive soft Scottish burr, the visitor knew exactly who spoke.

'Can I help you?' Sir Arthur Conan Doyle, sitting in his garden reading, his trusty hound by his side, saw someone for a fleeting second and moved towards the front of his house but could only see the back of the visitor.

As Herbert went to turn to face the man he came to see, and cop whatever rebuke was on offer, the door was opened by Major Wood.

'Mr Greenhough Smith,' said Wood. 'What a lovely surprise.'

'Good morning Major Wood. I apologise for calling unannounced but I come on a matter of great urgency.'

'I see,' said Wood feigning ignorance.

'Is Sir Arthur at home?'

'I'm not sure,' lied Wood trying to avoid a nasty scene. 'I thought I saw him slip out for his daily constitutional.'

'I thought I heard him a moment ago in the garden,' began the editor looking back to try and spy the now vanished author. 'Oh,' he said seeing no-one.

'I'll go and check for you, sir,' said Wood. 'In the meantime, why not examine Sir Arthur's latest acquisition?' Herbert looked blank. 'His new motor car is around the drive in front of the garage.'

Herbert knew a polite refusal waited in the wings. They both knew.

'Of course,' nodded the visitor and set off.

The secretary headed to Sir Arthur's study not exactly in fear and trembling but certainly without a spring in his step.

His employer bristled. 'The cheek of the fellow,' thundered Sir Arthur in an angry whisper. 'No appointment, my telegram could not have been more clear, and yet here he is, large as life and shameless.'

'He knows you're here, Sir Arthur.' That stopped the author's chagrin. 'He said he heard you in the garden.'

Sir Arthur blustered. 'Tell him he heard the gardener.'

'What, a Cornishman with a Scottish accent?'

'Tell him I'm unwell. Tell him I've died.'

The men stared at one another before Sir Arthur yielded.

'Oh all right. Show him in. But interrupt after five minutes with a reminder I have a speaking engagement this afternoon.'

'With whom?'

Arthur snapped, 'I don't know, anyone, The Mayor of Casterbridge. Just make up something.'

Herbert entered Sir Arthur's study where the host smiled and politely greeted the editor. These men went back a long way yet despite the bonhomie, an edge to the meeting crept in, a tension both could feel.

Greetings over, Sir Arthur, always a straight talker, cut to the chase.

'Now sir, let us come to the reason for your visit, this manuscript written by a woman calling herself Mrs Hudson.'

'Yes Sir Arthur, I ...'

'Her work, assuming it is hers, is another terrible pastiche, the sort I receive on a regular basis. Why a man of your experience would concern yourself with such third-rate piffle is beyond me.'

This strong opening statement left Herbert in no doubt as to the task ahead. But he'd spent hours planning tactics for this meeting. He knew a confrontational approach spelt danger but he chose to fight fire with fire.

'May I ask if you have read the *whole* manuscript, Sir Arthur?'

An excellent opening retort as both the question and combative approach from the visitor caused Sir Arthur to change tactics. He certainly changed his body language.

'I have read enough to know it is poor prose riddled with errors.'

'Ah,' replied Herbert. 'Errors being the key word, Sir Arthur. This is no ordinary pastiche. It lists the many mistakes in your work and, I confess, mistakes compounded by my unprofessional editing.'

The host snorted. 'Yes, yes; please come to the point.'

'I am ashamed at having allowed so many errors to remain uncorrected throughout your beautiful stories.'

The editor was relieved he threw in "beautiful stories", wanting desperately to win over the great man. But winning an argument counted for nothing if the editor couldn't locate Mrs Hudson and gain Sir Arthur's backing for the book.

'I admit, Greenhough Smith,' he said then stopped. 'I say, would you mind if I called you Smith?'

The editor wanted to say, "Not at all, Doyle" but wisely replied, 'Not at all, Sir Arthur.'

'You mention being ashamed at having been a poor editor, but I dispute there *are* such errors, and even if they do exist, surely they are of no consequence.'

Herbert played a dangerous game. He believed a gentle approach would see him shown the door leaving empty-handed. He chose to attack.

'But Sir Arthur, there is nothing so important as trifles.' The famous writer stiffened. 'And besides, your literary reputation is at stake here, sir.'

'Nonsense. My readers around the world care passionately about Sherlock Holmes. Few will even notice, let alone care about a few elementary mistakes. In fact, sir, I'm willing to wager readers in years to come will delight in spotting the occasional slip-up in my tales.'

Damn thought the visitor. *I've got him in a face-to-face meeting, in his home, but I'm still a million miles from winning his support.*

'If I may, Sir Arthur, I'd like to leave the manuscript with you.'

'No need, sir,' replied Sir Arthur.

Herbert persisted. 'I plan to republish your stories, sir, *without* the mistakes. I've marked the errors in the manuscript and would greatly appreciate you checking to see I haven't missed any.'

Ah, clever! Smart move, Herbert. That changed things and it piqued Sir Arthur's interest. 'Republish you say?'

'With every incorrect, misleading or unexplained point removed. I'm sure you'll be delighted with a new edition of your splendid stories. I was thinking of calling it a boxed set. Do you like the term?'

Sir Arthur endured discomfort. He hated Holmes but if his nitpicking critics could be silenced, it would be no bad thing. What could Sir Arthur say? 'If I have the time, I'll have a quick read.' He stood extending his hand. The meeting ended with Sir Arthur having not the slightest inclination to read the dreaded manuscript.

The editor sensed this and changed tactics. 'May I raise one other point, Sir Arthur?'

'Quickly.' Sir Arthur sat.

Herbert jumped in. He felt the tide turn in his favour. 'This woman's book reveals new characteristics about Holmes and Watson.'

'So she has a vivid imagination but there is no literary merit in her work. I repeat it's another of those tawdry pastiches which pop up everywhere. Imitation, Smith, is the sincerest form of flattery.'

Herbert was losing and went for the knock-out punch. Did he go too early? He threw caution to the wind. 'We can question the literary merit but there is no question about the potential of her manuscript to make a great deal of money.'

Ah, the old bribery ploy. Bullseye. It worked as the author froze. 'As you would know, Sir Arthur, excellence in literature is not always rewarded financially.'

Oops. That sounded wrong. The editor battled to clarify his statement. Sir Arthur wondered. *Have I just been insulted?* Did Sir Arthur's popular detective stories generate vast wealth despite their limited literary merit or, alternatively, are the Doylean historical novels great literature which struggle to make a quid?

The author wanted the editor gone and stood to dismiss the man. Herbert had his emergency tactic ready and produced the original document from his case.

'I have the original manuscript, Sir Arthur. May I explain why I'm confident it will become a highly successful commercial publication?'

That worked, for now, and Sir Arthur resumed his seat. His curiosity surged but not that you would know. He'd given the text scant attention when it arrived with its author. Now that a leading publisher and editor arrived with the material, the author became curious.

'What makes you think it could possibly be commercially successful?'

Herbert worked his magic, placing the manuscript on the desk and standing beside Sir Arthur. 'It's as if the woman calling herself Mrs Hudson really *is* the landlady at 221B Baker Street.'

Sir Arthur groaned. 'Oh please, Smith, you sound like one of those pathetic readers who believe Holmes and Watson are flesh and blood.'

'But Sir Arthur, consider these incidents.' Smith had placed strips of paper between the pages he wanted to display. 'Here is an example.' He read. 'Late one evening, a young woman called at Baker Street in great distress. Mr Holmes and Dr Watson had retired. In the darkened rooms, they dressed hurriedly and raced into the night to help the woman. Only when they reached her nearby residence did they realise both were wearing their dressing gowns.'

'Ridiculous, it never happened. I never wrote such a thing.'

'But it sounds plausible, Sir Arthur, and that's the key. So many anecdotes in her book are believable and interesting. She either has a vivid imagination or was actually in the building.'

'What building? There is no 221B Baker Street.'

The editor ignored his client. 'Mrs Hudson's jottings are an example of those "behind-the-scenes" snippets which readers of your Sherlockian stories are desperate to read.'

'She makes a penny dreadful read well. It's rubbish.'

'But rubbish sells, Sir Arthur, it sells.' He grunted his disdain. 'And now, because of the new copyright laws, you are entitled to a share of the income from the sale of Mrs Hudson's manuscript when it becomes a book.'

Sir Arthur stopped. He hadn't thought of that. He found the news intriguing but tried desperately to hide any sign of his mounting interest.

Herbert turned the pages. 'And over here, if I may,' he said. 'This is the shocking truth about Dr Watson's first wife, Mary Morstan. There,' he said, pointing, 'please read.'

Conan Doyle's impatience bubbled away but so too his fascination. Herbert persuaded. Sir Arthur read under protest but read he did and what he saw shocked him. 'That's outrageous. How could she know that?'

'You mean it's true?' gasped the visitor, trembling with excitement.

'I admit I considered the possibility of such an event but told no-one. This Mrs Hudson creature could never have known the detail.'

'But if Dr Watson's wife called at Baker Street and discussed the event, Mrs Hudson would have been witness to what happened.'

Sir Arthur's struggled. *The writer calling herself Mrs Hudson is a real person. I met her, here in this room. The landlady, Mrs Hudson, living at 221B Baker Street, a non-existent address, is not real!*

Herbert bit his lip. Sir Arthur failed to believe. The suspension of disbelief began to fade, and once lost, Sir Arthur would never accept this manuscript. Herbert had one final shot in his locker. Sir Arthur prepared to mock Mrs Hudson, her manuscript and Greenhough Smith himself. The editor threw his knockout punch.

'Mrs Hudson could have known all the details in her book if she believed in the spirit world.' Bang! Sir Arthur copped a thunderbolt. 'What if the Mrs Hudson who wrote this manuscript is a medium?'

Wow! Sir Arthur's head pounded. His belief in spiritualism was well known. He knew it to be the answer to the suffering of many disconsolate souls. He no longer attended patients with colds, injuries and diseases, but to those with a broken heart, he could prescribe a magnificent cure—communion with loved ones who have passed over.

Herbert moved in for the kill and whispered his sales pitch. 'If Mrs Hudson could contact Dr Watson's late wife, she, Mrs Hudson, could discover your plans for Mrs Watson's life.'

Sir Arthur couldn't believe Smith took any of this seriously. Mrs Watson, née Morstan was, *is* a fictional character in the stories he invented. Now a plot development he considered years ago but discarded is set out in perfect detail before his eyes. Sir Arthur made no notes of Mrs Watson's future and told no-one about his idea.

How the dickens could this Mrs Hudson character know my mind? Is she a medium? Can she read the mind of <u>living</u> people?

As he pondered these hitherto unimaginable questions, Wood knocked on the study door. He acted according to the specific instruction of his employer.

'I'm sorry to interrupt, Sir Arthur but I hope you haven't forgotten you are to deliver a speech this afternoon.'

The reaction was swift and loud. 'Get out, man, get out!' snapped Sir Arthur and a bewildered Major Wood retreated, his mind spinning. *What is going on with Sir Arthur?*

Doyle placed a hand on the manuscript. 'I'll give it a quick read, Smith.' The author stood; the meeting was over.

Herbert felt fantastic. He reckoned he'd hooked Sir Arthur Conan Doyle. The men shook hands and Herbert left the study. Waiting in the corridor, Major Wood tried to read the publisher's face.

'All good, Major Wood,' whispered Herbert as they walked to the front door. There they stopped.

'I'm worried, Mr Greenhough Smith,' said Wood. 'Your manuscript from this woman has caused Sir Arthur to react in a disturbing way.'

'He'll be fine, Major. Once we re-publish all his Sherlockian stories without the mistakes, he'll be a new man. Please encourage him to study the entire manuscript and help me get it into tip-top shape.'

'I'll do my best,' said Wood, still worried about his boss.

'But what I need is the full name and address of this Mrs Hudson woman. I'm sure Sir Arthur, with all his contacts, fame and influence can draw her out.'

'I'll see what I can do,' said Wood.

They shook hands. Walking the two miles back to Crowborough, Herbert had no idea if Mrs Hudson would ever be seen again.

Chapter 11

WATSON AND HOLMES dressed down with none of their fancy headgear, sweeping coats and expensive walking sticks or canes. They looked like a couple of retired chaps who once worked in a bank or for the Prudential Insurance Company. They were in the Strand maintaining a steady pace as if heading to Victoria Embankment on their lunch break before returning to their desks in the City.

'I see no sense in this, Holmes,' said Watson. 'The best way to stop Mrs Hudson's book being published is to persuade her to withdraw it.'

'You have failed to grasp the situation, Watson. The woman is not for turning. She thinks she has discovered a great truth about her famous tenants and moreover, she believes she is actually helping us by having her jottings circulated around the globe.'

Watson shook his head in despair. 'So why not forget it and her and retire. If she publishes, we won't be around to see it.'

'If she publishes, Watson, the world will beat a path to our door seeking a response to her incredible claims. The fourth estate today is obsessed with scandal. If you want a peaceful retirement, Mrs Hudson's book must never see the light of day.'

They turned into Burleigh Street and stopped opposite the office of *The Strand Magazine*.

'I hope you don't want me to go inside, Holmes. All my dealings with the editor have been through my literary agent.'

'Calm yourself, Watson.'

'I wouldn't know what to say and besides, if we, the subjects of the book, protest at it being published, surely our action will ensure the editor is even more determined to do exactly that.'

'Then we must be more determined. What time would you say the occupants depart the building? Do publishers burn the midnight oil?'

Watson paled. Across the road stood a building being studied by his friend; Watson twigged. 'Oh no, Holmes, you can't. You cannot even *think* about breaking into that building, *any* building. What if you're caught? Think of the shame, the damage to your reputation and illustrious career.'

'Watson, I would ask you to kindly use the correct pronoun.' The doctor's face appeared blank. 'What if *we're* caught, my good fellow?'

'Oh no—no, no, no.' Watson protested to himself as Holmes resumed their stroll causing his friend to hurry after him. When he caught up, Holmes explained the proposed nocturnal activity.

'There is a recess to the front door which will afford some privacy. I have every confidence in our little venture.'

'Please, Holmes, I beg you. Do not pursue this matter. There are other ways. What about the copyright law you mentioned last night?'

'Time, Watson; the wheels of justice grind ever so slowly. Urgent action is required, most urgent.'

'But breaking the law, Holmes; surely that is a step too far.'

'Come my dear fellow, it's not as if it's the first time.' Watson rolled his eyes. He would never win this argument.

They continued to stroll until they reached a tea-room. Watson made one final attempt to stop his friend doing the unthinkable.

'Holmes we are no longer young. You have rheumatic pain. My memory is not in top form. Our days of chasing criminals are over.'

'Speak for yourself,' he replied as the waitress arrived to take their order. When she left, Holmes spoke in a soft voice. 'I cannot believe you have forgotten the case with the Bruce-Partington plans.'

'Of course I remember. How could I forget?'

'And does the name Charles Augustus Milverton ring a bell?'

'But that was years ago involving serious criminal activity.'

'There are times when a simple burglary is essential and tonight is one such time.'

Watson grew angry and whispered. 'Holmes, we are not at war. No secret government documents are missing. A woman's reputation is not at stake.'

'No but our reputations are at stake; both our reputations.'

'Holmes, we *solve* crimes; we don't commit them.'

'Would you prefer we set fire to the building to save ourselves the trouble of breaking and entering?'

Watson pulled back to stop himself from shouting, which would have been most unusual for him, and especially in a public tea-room. Tea and cake arrived bringing a temporary halt to their "chat".

With refreshments in place, Watson resumed his objections. 'Why don't we find someone else to carry out the business?'

'Someone else?' asked Holmes tucking into a Victoria Sponge.

'What's wrong with those lads you paid to run errands and do a spot of spying?'

'You mean The Baker Street Irregulars.'

'They're the ones. Being young and nimble, they could be up the back stairs, in and out, grab the manuscript and be back at Baker Street before you can say Bertram Robinson.'

'Jack Robinson.'

'Pardon?'

'The saying is before you can say *Jack* Robinson.'

'What did I say?'

'Watson it doesn't matter because The Baker Street Irregulars are now middle-aged men and probably fathers with children the age they were when working for me.'

'Well how about them, the children of the Baker Street Irregulars? You might have to pay a little more but if they're half as good as their paters, our problem is solved.'

'Watson, I bumped into their leader, Wiggins, a few weeks ago. He recognised me. "Mr Holmes," he said. "How are you, sir? Still solving mysteries and catching criminals?" We enjoyed a few memories and then we parted.'

Watson desperately did not wish to finish his career as a burglar. 'Well why not ask him if he's interested?'

'Because we've both retired from solving crimes. The man's a respectable middle-aged shop-owner with a wife and four children.'

'Four children,' exclaimed Watson, begging Holmes to find an alternative method. 'Has he trained *them* in the business?'

'I asked him, Watson, half in jest, and he looked aghast and said, "Oh no Mr Holmes; we're regular worshippers at the Park Lane Methodist Church. The kiddies go to Sunday school. We're all God-fearing folk, Mr Holmes".'

Watson felt ill. His long and happy friendship with Sherlock Holmes appeared to be crumbling. They ate and drank in silence.

Holmes finished his tea, placed coins on the table, stood and left. Watson gulped the remainder of his tea, snatched the remaining Victoria Sponge and hurried after his friend.

A long night beckoned as the two ageing would-be burglars prepared to risk their reputations to save their reputations.

Back at Baker Street, Holmes continued to pack his belongings—slowly. He had planned to farewell London days ago but something unusual happened; a certain landlady and her manuscript being the unusual something. At the late hour, and as if on cue, she tapped on the sitting-room door and poked her head around same.

'Oh, you're still up, Mr Holmes.'

'Indeed Mrs Hudson and, as you have observed, still packing my belongings. But tell me, why are you not polishing your prose?'

'I've left my manuscript with Mr Greenhough Smith, entrusting him with the polishing.'

'So there is no copy of your manuscript here at Baker Street?'

'No, Mr Holmes, the only copy is stored securely at *The Strand Magazine*.' The landlady knew nothing of Herbert's copy.

But not for long thought Holmes.

'Did you say something, Mr Holmes?'

'Indeed I did not, madam.'

'Then I shall bid you goodnight, and be away to my bed.' She left, closing the door. Holmes placed some scientific equipment in the tea chest and moved to check a hold-all in which were hidden old-fashioned housebreaking implements. He glanced at his watch.

Holmes dressed for the cold and placed the housebreaking implements in the pockets of his heavy overcoat. Checking Mrs Hudson had indeed retired, in the deathly quiet building, he crept downstairs, slipped out the front door and into a deserted Baker Street. He walked towards The Regent's Park. If seen on this wet and dark street at this hour, Holmes would not be standing in front of his home address.

Fog would have been handy but instead healthy rain greeted Holmes who kept it at bay with a large umbrella. He looked along the street and saw a cab approach. It slowed then stopped.

'Good evening, sir,' said Watson and the detective climbed aboard.

They headed to Charing Cross station although trains at this hour were few and besides, the "lads" were not after engine numbers.

They walked along The Strand and turned left into Burleigh Street. The buildings were dark. The relatively new electric street lighting did a better job than the old gas lamps but even they struggled to challenge the darkness. With the persistent rain, it seemed a perfect night for our two enterprising burglars to go a-burgling.

They walked to the address and stepped into the recessed doorway and out of the rain. 'Holmes,' said Watson wanting to sneeze as water trickled down his neck, 'this is ridiculous. We're too old for adventure and even if we can affect an entry, we may not find the manuscript.'

'Your police lantern please, Watson; shine it here but stand behind so as to block any spillage.'

Holmes produced his set of skeleton keys and went to work. This was not the Bank of England and they heard a lock being opened.

'Kill the light, Watson and try not to wake the neighbours.'

They entered the corridor and crept to the first door in what could be described as India ink darkness. Holmes struck a match and read the sign, *The Strand Magazine*. Another lock to be unlocked and then they were inside Reception. Mrs Hudson handed over her manuscript in this office and now her tenants were intent on pinching her prose.

Stealing was not too powerful a word. This was common or garden theft. It worried Watson but the automaton called Holmes cared not a fig for his actions. He believed his landlady had betrayed him and, as for the errors in his many cases, blame there belonged to Watson or rather his literary agent and the editor of *The Strand Magazine*. Preventing the publication of the landlady's memoir was the right thing to do—absolutely.

'You search in here, Watson. I'll try elsewhere,' said Holmes who opened an inner door and disappeared. Watson used his old lamp but kept it on the floor beneath young Ernest Balfour's desk. Nothing resembling Mrs Hudson's masterpiece was found.

Ten minutes later Holmes returned. 'Anything, Watson?'

'Nothing.'

'Have you searched everywhere?'

'Everywhere except the kitchen sink.'

'What about the waste-paper bin?'

The silence sounded loud. Watson had failed—again. Holmes made a bee-line for the receptacle.

'Oh come now, Holmes, why would the manuscript be thrown in the rubbish?'

Holmes placed the contents of the basket on the desk. 'Some light please, Watson.' The good doctor obliged. Holmes studied each piece of paper until one grabbed his attention.

'Yes!'

'What is it?'

'A telegram from ...' The half-light made it tricky to read. '... Arthur Conan Doyle.'

'He's my literary agent,' said Watson.

'Well he and Mr Greenhough Smith have much to say about our landlady's literary adventure. If the manuscript is not here or at Baker Street, I've a good idea where it is.'

'Conan Doyle has the manuscript,' exclaimed Watson.

'Excellent, Watson; we'll make a detective out of you yet.'

'But we're doomed, Holmes. It's too late. I can already see the cover of next month's *Strand Magazine*.'

'Why would the manuscript be with your literary agent?'

'He would notate the errors; *our* errors.'

'Bravo, Watson, we are making progress.'

'Bravo? Holmes, without the manuscript, we cannot stop the work being published.'

'So we visit its new location and retrieve it.'

'*More* stealing? Oh Holmes, I would rather retire and be mocked than stand in the dock as a convicted felon.'

The agitated discussion hit the wall when noises in the street killed their conversation. 'The light, Watson, the light,' hissed Holmes.

It died and the men froze in the darkness. The door to the street rattled and then opened.

'Damn,' swore Holmes, 'the front door lock is not working. Hop under the desk, Watson,' said Holmes bending to hide.

'Hop?' he whispered having lost control of his beating heart.

Holmes crouched under young Ernest's desk. Watson knelt and struggled to join his friend. It proved a squeeze and grunts and groans erupted. Holmes said "shush", and the criminals held their breath as the door to Reception opened.

A light flashed around the room. 'Nothing,' said the first constable. 'Are you sure you saw a light?'

'I may have been mistaken. Nothing to steal here anyway,' said the other. 'Come on.'

The officers left providing terrific relief for the senior felons.

'Never again, Holmes,' muttered Watson crawling out from their hiding place. He stood and rubbed his elbow and elsewhere. 'Come on; let's leave before they come back.'

'I say, Watson, do be a sport, old fellow.'

Watson spat his reply. 'I am finished with this criminal behavior, Holmes. I never want to do this sort of thing again. Kindly do the right thing and retire. Forget Greenhough Smith and Conan Doyle and particularly Mrs Hudson's manuscript. Now please, come along.'

'I can't,' replied the detective.

'Can't?' snapped Watson. 'Crawl out as did I.'

Holmes groaned. 'Watson, it's my rheumatism.'

Chapter 12

AS HOLMES AND WATSON tried their hand at a spot of break and enter, Sir Arthur sat alone in his study. Family and staff were in bed as the author began reading that certain manuscript.

Despite the late hour, he felt no tiredness. His mind buzzed as he studied the material apparently written by a woman calling herself Mrs Hudson. It was explosive.

Of course the woman is a real person using a false name. But who is she and more to the point, how does she know so much intimate detail about my characters? Did I really make so many errors? And worst of all, why are her remarks all true?

He studied the mistakes she listed. He shook his head. 'It can't be right,' he said aloud. 'How did I miss that?' Then later, 'Why did I not remember that?'

Occasionally he would fetch a copy of the relevant *Strand Magazine* to check a detail. Sure enough, the alleged error was there in black and white, and the mistake as listed by Mrs Hudson was spot on. 'Damn the woman,' he muttered. Sometimes he found the so-called errors to be nitpicking but still the pressure built.

'Oh really,' he snapped. 'It's circumstantial evidence; not an error.'

His despair expanded. Sherlock Holmes was a hit around the world, and yet, according to a woman named Mrs Hudson—what an appalling joke that is—these wildly popular mysteries are packed, not dotted but crammed with unexplained events, silly mistakes and factual errors.

Why didn't that damn editor tell me geese don't have a crop?

Depression gripped him. If this manuscript were to ever see the light of day, he envisaged his brilliant career ending in ignominy. Thoughts pinged inside his head.

Is this the only copy of the manuscript? What if a terrible accident occurred? A fire? What if the Royal Mail lost the package which I definitely asked my secretary to return?

A wicked thought popped into his brain. The author planned a shocking crime. His conscience sent off a distress flare. He ignored it. Without hesitation he picked up the manuscript, shoved it into his jacket pocket and headed outside. His conscience formed a percussion band. The moon hid. His dog insisted on tagging along. Midnight rambles were the best. Sir Arthur decided. With matches in his pocket, he would turn the pages to ash.

At the bottom of his garden he collected fallen twigs and leaves. He made a pile, a pyre upon which he would save his honour and legacy. His pooch whined his concern. Voices in Sir Arthur's head shouted, demanding he desist. He ignored them.

If this book is published, I will be mocked. My work in explaining spiritualism will be thwarted. Being a laughing stock will destroy my Pauline mission to promote the spirit world.

The wind took a breather. In the darkness he struck a match and lit the leaves and twigs. They failed to light. He took the manuscript from his jacket pocket and tore off the frontispiece. Scrunching the page into a ball, he pushed it in amongst the twigs and lit another match. This time brought success. Using a stick, he maneuvered the twigs and soon crackling flames began to dance.

Sir Arthur appeared devilish in the firelight. Was he already in Hell? He gathered more twigs and fed the flames. He wanted serious heat to engulf the manuscript. No slow burn, no insipid destruction; he wanted fierce and all-consuming glory.

The dog barked and his master reprimanded the hound. The canine reckoned this new caper could be dangerous, a threat to his beloved leader. His jumping and barking dominated.

Sir Arthur wanted the matter settled now, once and for all. He withdrew the manuscript preparing to thrust it into the heart of the fire. The dog went crazy.

'Arthur!' cried a voice. It sounded distressed and on the move. 'Is that you, Arthur,' cried his wife who, with a shawl wrapped around her nightdress, came running through the garden.

The dog became even more excited and Sir Arthur panicked. He stood centre stage being attacked by a yelling wife and a barking dog, as he prepared to carry out a cultural crime, an act of barbarism. It became a different kind of curious incident of the dog in the night-time. He stopped. The manuscript he wished to destroy got shoved back inside his jacket and his boots stamped on the fire as his good lady arrived.

'Arthur, what's happening?' she cried in fear.

'It's nothing to worry about, my dear. Just an experiment for my latest story,' he said as sparks from the scattered twigs danced in the darkness.

Over the last few days, Sir Arthur's second wife, Jean, worried about her husband's behavior and this event made it worse. When she asked about his health, he dismissed her concerns. Lady Conan Doyle remained unconvinced, especially now after this backyard blaze. At the first opportunity, she would discuss her husband's behavior with his secretary.

The dog settled and all three returned to the house. Mrs Hudson's manuscript, sans frontispiece, re-appeared on Sir Arthur's desk.

That same night, Herbert Greenhough Smith also worried. Like Sir Arthur, Herbert became Mr Anxiety proving that under pressure, educated and successful men can behave erratically. Sir Arthur tried to burn the book; Herbert tried to burn the midnight oil.

He read the only copy of Mrs Hudson's manuscript again. He wished he'd asked his assistant to include the handwritten notes Mrs Hudson made in the margins; they added so much. But the text itself held him spellbound. He reckoned it to be a guaranteed bestseller.

Getting Sir Arthur to back the title would be a huge coup. When he left the author, Herbert reckoned the great man might have conceded. No guarantee but certainly Sir Arthur's endorsement could happen.

But then Herbert's depression deepened. Yes, he had the manuscript, with luck the support of the famous creator of Sherlock Holmes, and clearly the blessing of Mrs Hudson the author. But horror of horrors, he didn't have her. She vanished and worse, no-one knew where. Nobody even knew her first name.

Welcome to my nightmare. The editor was so close to success and yet so far. Herbert hoped Sir Arthur might find her. But why? The famous author had incentive to never find her.

'Think, man, think,' said Herbert to himself as he listed ideas to find Mrs Hudson. Some ideas seemed ridiculous, *were* ridiculous, such as spreading a rumour a firm of solicitors was seeking a woman known as Mrs Hudson as she had been left a sizeable fortune from her recently deceased great Aunt. The woman's age, height, weight, hair colour would be listed and, of course, they matched those of Mrs Hudson.

Other ideas were newspaper notices, letters to fans, and a visit to the police. 'My God,' he whispered, 'people will think me insane.'

He drafted two newspaper notices. The first for *The Times* established a tone of respect in which a member of the establishment was keen to make contact with an estranged relative. A family reunion was sought and soon because of the advanced age of the family matriarch. The estranged family member called herself Mrs Hudson.

The notice sparked animated conversations around aristocratic dining tables with folk keen to guess the family involved.

The second notice would appear in the *Daily Herald*, an organ aimed at the lower classes. Herbert knew the readership of London's publications. Here the notice in the *Personal Columns* appealed to more ignoble human instincts. Mrs Hudson had been left a sizeable legacy and anyone helping locate her—description followed—would receive a handsome reward—20 guineas.

Herbert prayed, hoped his notices would work.

His desperation drove him to consider Sherlock Holmes. Of course he knew Holmes, Watson and their landlady were fictional characters; but he met a woman calling herself Mrs Hudson who produced the manuscript, a copy of which currently sat on his desk. Now if "his" Mrs Hudson is a keen follower of the fictional Holmes and Watson, then readers know other readers.

Maybe my Mrs Hudson belongs to a reading group who appreciate Sir Arthur's tales. Of course, that's it; find Mrs Hudson via her friends. Readers of Sherlock Holmes will surely know her.

He searched letters from readers of *The Strand Magazine*. He wanted the address of the most fervent local followers. If Mrs Hudson is local, local readers will know her, and they can be easily reached.

Herbert felt like a political candidate about to go door knocking canvassing for votes. He felt like Sherlock Holmes, sifting through evidence to uncover the perpetrator of a crime. Excitement built. Thankfully, for his own health and wellbeing, Herbert tended to be a glass half full kind of person.

With his list complete, he put it to one side ready for his search to begin in the morning. The bewitching hour drew nigh. But despite the lateness, stopping work was not on Herbert's agenda. He donned his coat and slipped out the front door.

Chapter 13

PADDINGTON GREEN POLICE STATION was on Herbert's way home, and its bright blue light shone in the dark. The station was certainly open and manned because the Metropolitan Police sent far more men out on patrol at night than during the day. It was something to do with criminals craving darkness. Herbert approached the front counter.

'Good evening, sir,' said Constable Anderson. 'How can we help?'

'I wish to report a missing person.'

'Certainly, sir,' said the constable searching for the correct form. 'Now, can I have the name of the missing person?'

'Hudson.'

The constable began writing. 'Hudson. First name?'

'Mrs.'

The constable looked at Herbert. 'No sir, her first name.'

'Not known,' said Herbert maintaining his serious demeanour.

'Not known, sir? You wish to report a missing person whose name you do not know?'

'Please, officer, allow me to explain.'

'It's just that we have hoaxers in here, sir, as well as folk who are, shall we say, confused. If this lady is a genuine missing person ...'

'She is. I swear she is a genuine lost soul.'

The constable became even more suspicious. The words "lost soul" suggested a religious component. The woman was not physically missing; it was her faith that had disappeared. Besides, the police had enough on their hands without worrying about backsliders.

Anderson stopped writing and waited for the time-waster to repair the huge credibility gap in his story. Herbert explained.

'The other day I met a lady who introduced herself as Mrs Hudson. She came to my office at *The Strand Magazine* in central London. I'm Herbert Greenhough Smith, the editor of the magazine. Actually she made two visits. On the second, she entered my office and we spoke at length about a manuscript she wrote.'

The editor paused, assessing the constable to try and gauge his response.

'Go on, sir,' said Constable Anderson, waiting to be convinced.

'She left and when my staff tried to find her, she'd disappeared.'

'How do you mean, disappeared?'

'She wasn't outside in the street, and the address she gave doesn't exist.'

'But if she came to your office and presented a manuscript you found interesting, wouldn't you normally take her details, her name and address?'

'Of course.'

'I mean if you came in here to report a missing person, would you find it strange if I didn't write down the missing person's details?'

'Of course,' repeated Herbert now growing frustrated.

'Well, sir, I think it's strange you wanting to report a missing person you've only met once and ...'

'Twice. She came back a second time.'

'And whose name you don't know.'

'I know her surname.'

'But nothing else.' Herbert's spirits slumped.

The constable had heard enough. The man may have been well-dressed, well-spoken and well-meaning but based on the details provided; this so-called Mrs Hudson was likely a figment of Mr Greenhough Smith's imagination.

'I'm sorry, sir,' said the constable. 'We'd like to help but without the missing lady's name and address, there's not much we can do.'

Herbert despaired. 'Oh Constable, please, it's vital we find her. It's most definitely to her advantage if we do.'

'But not to your advantage, sir?'

He hesitated. 'Well, yes, but the world will lose some invaluable information about a famous and much-loved person, and miss out on the answers to questions they would love to resolve if we can't locate this lady.'

The constable shook his head. 'You've lost me, sir. I haven't got the foggiest idea what you're talking about.'

Herbert despaired. His plea for help failed. Dismissal time beckoned. *Thank you and goodnight, sir* is what the constable meant.

Herbert hesitated then decided. He had no choice. He would tell the truth as crazy as it would sound. The police wouldn't help so one might as well go the whole hog. *Anyway, what can they do? Laugh me out of the station?* Herbert went for it.

'Constable, the missing Mrs Hudson is the landlady of the world famous detective, Mr Sherlock Holmes.'

End of speech, end of explanation, end of visit to police station. Herbert prepared to turn and leave with the policeman catcalling and laughing as the editor fled the station.

A pause then Constable Anderson gave Herbert an almighty spray. 'Well why didn't you say so in the first place?' He called. 'Sarge, Sarge, come in here, now!'

A senior officer appeared wiping digestive biscuit crumbs from his face and uniform. 'What's happened, Constable?'

'This gentleman's the editor of *The Strand Magazine*.'

'Herbert Greenhough Smith,' said Herbert offering his hand to the sergeant who shook it.

'How do,' said Sergeant Coventry.

'And Sarge, he has terrible news about a missing person.'

'Who?' asked the now alarmed Sergeant.

'Mrs Hudson,' said Greenhough Smith without thinking.

The Sergeant blanched. 'Not Mrs Hudson from 221B Baker Street?'

'Yes sir, the same,' said Herbert who struggled to understand the reaction from the two officers.

'*The* Mrs Hudson?' repeated the senior officer.

'Yes, Sarge,' said his constable, 'Mr Holmes' landlady.'

Coventry's face crumpled. Tears came to his eyes. 'But this is awful. How will Mr Holmes cope?'

'And Doctor Watson?' added Anderson.

Herbert joined their distress. 'Indeed and it's a particularly awkward time as Mr Holmes is about to retire.'

'What!?' yelled both officers who, in shock, spoke as one.

'Mr Holmes is leaving Baker Street?' asked Coventry.

'Yes, Sergeant,' said Herbert, caught up in the high emotion.

'For good?' almost begged Anderson.

'For good,' replied Herbert.

'The best detective in the whole world is quitting?' asked Coventry.

'Yes and that's why we need to find Mrs Hudson,' replied Herbert. 'If Mr Holmes leaves without the wonderful landlady to help him pack, he could forget all sorts of things.'

'His pipe and slippers,' said Coventry.

'His magnifying lens and violin,' said Anderson.

Sergeant Coventry barked an order. 'Constable, fetch Inspector Lestrade—now!'

The constable rushed out and Herbert struggled to believe the unfolding events but so desperate was he to find the missing landlady, he seized on the reaction of the police.

'I can give you an accurate description of Mrs Hudson, Sergeant.'

'Excellent, sir,' he said grabbing a pencil preparing to write. Before Herbert spoke, the Sergeant made a request. 'I don't suppose you have a photo of Mrs Hudson?'

Herbert hesitated. 'I'm afraid I don't. No, wait! I probably have an illustration drawn by Mr Sidney Paget.'

The officer beamed. 'Oh that would be perfect, sir. Will Mr Paget sign the drawing?'

Herbert became emotional. 'Ah, sadly Mr Paget has passed away but he always initialled his drawings.'

The Sergeant announced with pride. 'I have all of Mr Paget's illustrations, sir. It would an honour to add Mrs Hudson to my collection.'

Herbert struggled to stay sane. 'I'm impressed, Sergeant.'

'Several of the lads here are great collectors of the memorabilia of the cases of Mr Holmes.'

Herbert found himself floating in and out of reality. He knew what day (night) it was, his location, and why he came to the police station. He knew the late Sidney Paget, the fine illustrator, was a real person, and Herbert knew the officer standing in front of him must be real. But some of the actions and comments in this station in the last few minutes were, well, unusual. As he attempted to sort fact from fantasy, several officers burst in including Inspector Lestrade.

'What's this I hear, Sergeant?' demanded Lestrade. 'Mrs Hudson's been murdered. This is terrible. Mr Holmes will be devastated.'

Herbert panicked. 'No, not murdered,' he cried.

'Missing, Inspector,' said his sergeant. 'She's only missing. And this gentleman is the editor of *The Strand Magazine*.

'Thank heavens,' said the Inspector. 'I know the dear lady from my many visits to 221B Baker Street, but the general public may not know her. They don't even know her first name.'

'Nobody does,' added Herbert.

The Sergeant explained. 'We're getting an illustration drawn by Mr Sidney Paget. And it will be signed.'

'Initialled,' said Herbert with his comment ignored by the excited officers. 'And I think it's only a preliminary sketch.'

'Wonderful,' said the Inspector, 'I don't think I've got that one.' Lestrade turned to Herbert who felt an urge to pinch himself. 'I once heard, sir, you offered the illustrator's position to Mr Sidney Paget's brother, Walter. Is there any truth in that, sir?'

Herbert did pinch himself. 'I don't usually discuss confidential business matters, sir, but I would not be lying if I were to say there is more than a grain of truth in such a tale.' The police officers grinned.

'I told you so,' said Constable Anderson to a colleague.

Herbert entertained his fascinated audience. 'The story goes that Sidney stole his brother's job offer and obtained the role of illustrator working for my magazine. By way of restitution, he used his brother Walter as a model for Mr Holmes. It was a great likeness.'

The police buzzed. This gripping news came straight from the horse's mouth. Herbert's audience hung on his every word.

Constable Anderson buttonholed the editor. 'I heard a story, although I can't verify it, that Walter Paget went to the theatre one evening, and as he made his way to his seat, another theatregoer pointed to him and exclaimed, "Look, there goes Sherlock Holmes".'

'Possibly,' replied Herbert. 'There are many stories about Mr Holmes.'

What a tale. It would do the rounds of the police station and beyond for days, even weeks.

Sergeant Coventry took control. 'Well come along, gentlemen, this won't help us find Mrs Hudson.' The officers dispersed with the Inspector warmly shaking hands with Herbert.

'I'm most grateful, Inspector,' said the editor.

'Least we could do, sir for such an important lady. I'll drop into Baker Street as soon as I can, sir. Cheerio.' He left, buzzing.

Herbert spoke to the Sergeant. 'I'll have the illustration delivered to you first thing tomorrow, officer.'

'And we'll pass the word to the men on patrol tonight to keep a sharp lookout for Mrs H.'

'Thank you, Sergeant and good night.'

'Goodnight, sir.'

Herbert staggered into Harrow Road and wondered what on Earth had happened to him in the last two days, and especially the last two hours. Was it Byron who said, "Truth is strange, indeed stranger than fiction"?

Herbert thought of that quote and spoke aloud. 'If only I knew the difference.'

Chapter 14

LIFE TURNED GRIM AT WINDLESHAM MANOR. Everything revolved around Sir Arthur, the patriarch and business manager. Everyone followed his orders, requests and wishes. When he was off his game, the entire team suffered.

Major Alfred Wood had worked for his friend Conan Doyle for decades, and in all that time, Wood had never seen the famous author so low. The reason, clearly, pointed in one direction—Mrs Hudson's manuscript. Ignoring it didn't work. Confronting it didn't work. Wood needed an idea, a circuit-breaker, something extraordinary to rescue his boss from his Slough of Despond.

Wood made his way to Sir Arthur's study dreading another display of anger and frustration. He wondered if the poisoned chalice, the manuscript, had been returned or, dare he think it, destroyed. Little did Wood know, a few hours ago, the document was seconds from destruction.

He knocked gently on the open door and felt enormous relief when he spied Mrs Hudson's tome on the desk. Wood wanted to be positive, to keep Sir Arthur thinking good thoughts, and steer him clear of depression. He didn't need to. Something had happened.

Sir Arthur looked up with a smile to delight the secretary. 'Good morning Woodie,' he said waving a letter. 'At last some good news.'

'Excellent, Arthur, and long may it reign.'

'Read this,' said the author handing Wood the note. As he studied the contents, his eyes grew larger. What a change of fortune.

The depression caused by the many errors listed in Mrs Hudson's manuscript, were all to do with the cases starring Sherlock Holmes. Mrs Hudson made no reference to Sir Arthur's historical novels. It appeared she knew nothing about them. And why should she? Mrs Hudson knew Dr Watson recorded the cases solved by Mr Holmes. Dr Watson never wrote an historical novel in his life. Dr Doyle on the other hand whipped out half a dozen or more.

And they were the subject of this letter. It was written on quality note paper with the letterhead of the Northumberland Hotel in London; the same hotel Holmes and Watson visited in *The Hound of the Baskervilles.*

'Ah,' said Wood, 'one of your favourite hostelries, Arthur.'

'Indeed,' he replied, feeling a new sense of happiness and pride in his work, missing since the arrival of *that* manuscript. 'Read on.'

Northumberland Hotel
Northumberland Avenue, London

August 29

Dear Sir Arthur

Permit me to introduce myself. I am Professor Heinrich Roth, head of the Department of English Literature at Leipzig University in Germany.

I have long been an admirer of your historical novels and in particular Micah Clarke, The White Company, Rodney Stone and Sir Nigel.

It is, I believe, a great pity your detective stories are given priority in literary circles when it is your historical novels which are important works of literature.

Would it be possible to have the opportunity to peruse the research notes of even one of your magnificent historical novels? I plan to include several in my teaching syllabus during the forthcoming academic year.

93

Wood returned the letter. 'My word, Arthur, you deserve many congratulations and what a coup. This sounds promising.'

'Promising? Woodie, this is what I've waited for my entire writing life. This is the best news I could ever hope for—recognition of my historical novels by academia.' He picked up then dropped Mrs Hudson's manuscript. 'This lightweight material means nothing to me. My detective stories have brought me riches but not the serious recognition I crave. Who cares if Holmes made the odd error? The recognition of my serious writing is all that matters. Only my historical novels count. Now, at long last the wheel has turned.'

He went to a bookshelf and selected a copy of *Micah Clarke*. 'This is some of my best writing. This is what intelligent readers appreciate, and now it will be part of a university's syllabus; the first of many.' His smile grew larger. 'This is just the start, Woodie. Soon the world will discover my true writing genius.'

Wood wanted to jump for joy. He and Lady Conan Doyle were worried sick about Arthur's depression, his anger following the discovery of the Hudson manuscript. Now, an academic emerged with a dazzling request. For Sir Arthur, life headed skywards.

'Send this Professor a telegram. Tell him he's welcome at any time.'

'It will have to be tomorrow, Arthur.'

'Tomorrow?' queried the shocked author. 'Why tomorrow?'

'He returns to Germany the day after. He said so in his letter.'

'Damn,' snapped the disappointed author. 'I have a speaking engagement tomorrow in Hastings. Jean and the children are coming. They're spending the day at the seaside. How can I cancel the trip?'

'You can't, Arthur, not without letting down many of your followers. You could invite the Professor to visit the next time he's in England.'

Sir Arthur flustered. 'No, no, no, I need to give him every support *now*. I've waited years for the writing establishment to recognize my historical novels. He must be invited. You'll be here, Woodie. Give him the run of the library.'

'If that's what you want, Arthur, of course I'll look after him.'

'And please do so now. Send a telegram to the Northumberland. Professor Roth arrives tomorrow.'

Sir Arthur felt renewed energy. He rubbed his hands together, his happiness, nay glee, out on show. 'I wonder if the Professor is a member of the Red-Headed League.'

Woodie frowned. 'I'm sorry, Arthur, you've lost me.'

'His name, man, his name; in German, Roth is a nickname for someone with red hair. If ever there was a good omen, Woodie, this is it.'

The Major gave a forced smile in response to the joy on the face of Sir Arthur. 'I'll send the telegram right away,' said Wood and left.

Chapter 15

SEVERAL PEOPLE WERE DESPERATE TO FIND MRS HUDSON. Herbert Greenhough Smith, obviously, and then the Metropolitan Police and, of course, Sherlock Holmes all wanted to locate the lady.

Herbert created newspaper notices and wrote letters while the Metropolitan Police made enquiries up and down Baker Street. Holmes feared he had no control over Mrs Hudson or what she would do with her manuscript so racked his brain for a plan. He alone had no strategy—as yet.

Herbert trawled though the box of Sidney Paget drawings and found a preliminary sketch of Mrs Hudson. He forged Sidney's initials without a second thought. Remarkably, the sketch bore a striking resemblance to the old woman who called at *The Strand*.

Herbert needed copies of the Paget sketch for his letter writing campaign. He sent young Ernest Balfour to the police station with the sketch where it scored excellent reviews from the new shift as well as from the officers who arrived later that night. Some clever copper produced a MISSING PERSON notice using Sidney's sketch, with copies printed and circulated. Some were rushed to the office of *The Strand Magazine*. The hunt began in earnest to find the creator of the inside story of the lives of Holmes and Watson.

Herbert wrote to several London-based readers who had written to *The Strand Magazine* expressing delight with the stories of Holmes and Watson mentioning the sterling work done by Mrs Hudson. These correspondents, always female readers, soon received a letter from Herbert.

The newspaper ads in *The Times* and *Daily Herald* produced a bag of replies, not surprising because *Herald* readers were offered cash should they find the missing scribe. Mind you, a million replies counted for nothing if no-one could locate Mrs H. No-one could.

Same too for the individual letters; not one reader produced the mystery author. Several knew a fellow reader who matched the description of Mrs Hudson but, when followed up, t'was not *the* Mrs Hudson. Nine readers stated they owned a cat called Sherlock with one claiming a parrot called Watson who could squawk *elementary*.

Now this whole search proved silly and unnecessary because the missing person wasn't missing. There she dwelt, the real Mrs Hudson, landlady and writer, as large as life at 221B Baker Street, where she continued to try and help her famous tenant get a wriggle on. She wasn't hiding or missing. She lived where she had lived forever. If only Herbert and the police had bothered to check.

'Still packing, Mr Holmes,' said Mrs Hudson bringing him a morning cup of tea. 'If I didn't know better, I'd think you were delaying your departure in order to prevent my memoir from ever being published.'

'You flatter yourself, Mrs Hudson. And does it not disturb you that your publisher and literary agent have not been to see you?'

'You know that, do you sir? You have remained here ever since I unveiled my little publishing venture all those nights ago?'

Smack! Again she outwitted him. The men he mentioned could easily have called at Baker Street while he was out.

A new and worrying thought occurred to Holmes. *How might my cases have gone if I'd worked with the landlady and not the lodger?*

He fell silent and she filled the gap. 'I think you'll find, Mr Holmes, they are waiting for my signal.'

Her one-upmanship continued. Ever since she stunned her tenant by revealing her manuscript, the great detective played catch up. Mrs Hudson evaded every jab from Holmes only to counter-punch with a stinging points-scoring blow.

'I've brought some tea, Mr Holmes. Shall I pour?'

'No thank you, madam. There are still some tasks I am able to perform *without mistake.*' The emphasis on the last two words highlighted Holmes' frustration. His bitterness simmered, a bit like the tea. She nodded and started to leave. He spoke and she stopped by the door. 'I am sorry we are going to part company on such an unpleasant note, Mrs Hudson.'

'Unpleasant, Mr Holmes? I am sad to see you go and have nothing but admiration for you as a brilliant detective and as a gentleman; at times shall we say eccentric but always unfailingly polite.'

She fought anger with peace and understanding. He gave one of his seemingly contrived smiles. She often thought about his sense of humour. When he laughed, she considered it harsh and short lived. His merriment was brief; Holmes the cut-off comic.

'I have learnt more about you, madam, in these last few days than in the decades I've spent under your roof here in Baker Street.'

'One should always be learning, sir. If I remember correctly, I think you once said, "education never ends".'

He winced again as she continued to reply using his own words. Still he strove for the upper hand. 'But disingenuous is not a word I would have associated with my landlady.' Now he addressed her in the third person.

'Goodness, Mr Holmes, I will have to consult a dictionary to follow your line of thinking.'

'And to disingenuous I might well add patronizing.'

Oh dear, talk about harsh. He regretted it as did she. The silence grew loud. She opened the door and turned. 'Don't let your tea get cold, Mr Holmes.' She left.

Furious, he continued packing. Pressure continued to build. Holmes, a proud man, some would say arrogant, knew his record, his achievements were his legacy but Mrs Hudson's claims nagged him. She created an itch no amount of scratching could remove.

Being accurate, being correct, being sure and never guessing were qualities to which he aspired; which he practised. When someone came along and exposed a plethora of mistakes and undermined his status, then bewilderment was the result.

Holmes was bewildered, a rare if unknown experience. And when the source of the claims against him came from such an unexpected source then his befuddlement only increased. But worse, far worse; he now came to believe the accusations against him were true.

Honesty ruled his life and he knew he'd been caught out. He couldn't deny it. Meet Polonius Holmes. *To thine own self be true.*

He poured tea, stood by the window above a busy Baker Street, sipped, and pondered his next move. It was rare, very rare for anyone to outwit Sherlock Holmes.

Chapter 16

THE GERMAN PROFESSOR DAY ARRIVED. Sir Arthur collected his notes for the lecture in Hastings, and helped his children with their seating arrangements in the car. Wood prepared his tasks for the day but stopped when Lady Conan Doyle entered his office.

'Woodie, I must speak with you,' she whispered. 'Arthur's behavior is getting worse. Surely you must have noticed.'

Wood agreed. 'I have, Jean, but it's not worse; it's much worse.'

'Last night I got a terrible fright. Around midnight I heard the dog barking. Through my bedroom window I saw a fire at the bottom of the garden.'

Wood worried. He knew nothing of this incident. 'A fire?'

She kept checking to see her husband wasn't in the corridor.

'It wasn't massive, more like a camp fire. I could see Arthur and the dog. I couldn't imagine what he was doing so late at night. I ran downstairs and into the garden. When I got closer I called to him. By the time I arrived, Arthur was stamping on the fire and had put it out. Naturally I asked him about it and he prattled on about conducting an experiment for one of his new books.'

'I have no idea what that could be,' said Wood, concerned.

'Woodie, I think he tried to burn something. Does that make any sense?'

'Possibly.'

'Possibly? What's going on, Woodie?'

He noticed Mrs Hudson's manuscript on Sir Arthur's desk. Something looked different but thankfully, it was still there.

'I'm still not sure about the fire,' said Jean. She handed him a charred piece of paper. 'I went out early this morning and found this near where Arthur lit the fire.'

Wood recognized the remains of the frontispiece of Mrs Hudson's manuscript. He began to explain when a voice rang out.

'Jean, where are you? We're late.'

Wood stuffed the burnt page in his jacket pocket as Sir Arthur arrived.

'Just checking with Woodie about your German visitor, my dear,' she said. 'You know how precise and particular our European cousins can be.' She left.

The two men exchanged glances. Sir Arthur suspected nothing of the conversation between his wife and secretary because all his thoughts were about the visitor he so desperately wanted to meet.

'This chap is important, Woodie.'

'I know, Arthur. I'll make him welcome and give him everything he needs.'

Sir Arthur thanked his man and left. Wood followed him to the car and waved the family farewell. He went back inside feeling glad to be able to work uninterrupted. But various issues troubled him.

Did Arthur try to destroy the manuscript? Did Jean's sudden arrival stop him? And will this German academic's visit be of any benefit to one clearly distressed author?

Wood set to work enjoying the freedom of an absent Arthur when, a few minutes later, he heard the car arriving. 'Oh damn,' he said, 'it's an emergency and they've turned back.' Then another thought occurred to Wood, a troubling thought. *Arthur has faked a problem so as to return and meet the visiting academic.*

He went to greet Sir Arthur and as he stepped out to the driveway, he stopped in surprise. The handsome Wolseley Model 20 Colonial Tourer Cylinder parked in the driveway most definitely did not belong to Sir Arthur.

Wood twigged. Of course; this is the visiting German Professor who is early. Instinctively the secretary stepped forward and opened the driver's door. Oh dear. Unless the Professor doubled as a chauffeur, this gent could not possibly be the learned lad from Leipzig.

The driver wore the traditional outfit—grey jacket and jodhpurs, black gloves and boots with a peaked black cap. No spring chicken, he chose the silent method of communication.

'Good morning,' said Wood. 'Professor Roth?'

The passenger door opened and a gentleman stepped out. 'Guten Tag, Sir Arthur. How do you do?' He spoke perfect English with a pronounced German accent.

Wood recovered and the two men set off in different directions—the professor walked via the front of the vehicle, and Wood via the rear—meaning it took longer for them to unscramble the faux pas and finally meet face to face and shake hands. Stifled guffaws ensured.

The tall, thin visitor was immaculately attired having velvet lapels on his jacket, with half-length trousers married to his long black socks. His bow-tie made a subtle statement as did his goatee beard and moustache both trimmed with military precision. The ribbon attached to his monocle looked to be more expensive than the actual eye glass. His headgear even featured a feather.

He gushed. 'I cannot tell you what an honour it is to meet so great a writer, Sir Arthur.'

Wood felt compelled to interrupt. 'Professor, please, I must tell you I am not Sir Arthur.'

Shock and disappointment appeared on Roth's face. He'd been so looking forward to this meeting for months, years, and to finally arrive and greet the wrong man, set the German back on his heels.

'I am Major Wood, Sir Arthur's friend and secretary.'

'Oh, how do you do, Major Wood?'

'Sir Arthur is profoundly sorry but he has a speaking engagement which he simply had to honour. He asked me to welcome you and give you every assistance with your research into Sir Arthur's historical novels.'

'Oh dankeschön, Major Wood. How kind you are.'

Wood indicated the house. 'Come this way, Professor.' The academic moved but the chauffer stood by the vehicle awaiting orders. 'And your man; is he to stay or return to collect you later?'

'Ah, this is *my* Major Wood. Schmidt is my driver and my, how do you English say, my general factotum?'

'Excellent,' smiled Wood and led the Professor inside. Schmidt followed carrying his employer's briefcase and overcoat.

Wood showed Professor Roth Sir Arthur's study and then led the visitor and his assistant to the library. Boxes sat on the table and Wood explained how Sir Arthur wanted all his manuscripts and notes to be placed at the professor's disposal.

'This is most generous of Sir Arthur,' said Roth. 'I will make a start immediately, if it is convenient.'

'It is, Professor. The lavatory is down the corridor to your right and I will have tea brought for you directly.'

'You are too kind, Major.'

Wood headed for the door. 'My office is next to Sir Arthur's study so please let me know if you require anything else. Oh, and good hunting.'

He smiled and left. The Professor looked around the library and then at his man Friday. Schmidt awaited instructions. His boss spoke in an English accent and whispered.

'Right, Watson, you start on those boxes. I'm after the important hidden material.'

Wood carried on oblivious to the fact two imposters—were they spies?—busied themselves in Sir Arthur's home. Watson, as usual well drilled by his friend, and Holmes were there to uncover something, anything which might help prevent the publication of Mrs Hudson's manuscript thereby saving their reputations.

'Tell me again, Holmes. What *exactly* should I look for?'

'You'll know when you find it.'

Watson's frustration bubbled away. 'That sounds like something a second-rate detective would say,' he said removing the contents of the first of Sir Arthur's boxes.

Holmes searched elsewhere. With no interest in historical novels, he wanted detective tales, those about him, written by Watson and sent to Doyle the literary agent. Holmes opened drawers, withdrew folders and searched.

'Watson,' whispered Holmes, 'remember only *your* writing counts. Forget those historical tales, and concentrate only on *your* writing.'

Watson grunted and searched. After a while, he tossed notes about archery in Medieval times on the table. 'Oh this is hopeless, Holmes. I couldn't write this boring claptrap. No wonder it's unheard of.'

Holmes moved to Watson to calm his friend. As he reached him, the visitors froze when a knock sounded, the door opened, and the housekeeper arrived with a tray.

'Good morning, gentlemen,' she said. 'Major Wood asked me to bring tea.'

Holmes greeted her. 'Guten Tag, dear lady und dankeschön. You are most kind.'

'I'll leave it here. Please do help yourselves.'

'Excuse me,' said Holmes, stopping the woman, 'but is your name by any chance Mrs Hudson?'

The housekeeper shook her head. Watson shook nothing having no idea why his friend would ask such a question.

'No, sir; I be Mrs Turner.'

Holmes persisted. 'Back in Germany, I have the stories about Sherlock Holmes been reading, and I thought his housekeeper they called Mrs Hudson.'

'That's right, sir but Mrs Hudson and Sherlock Holmes live in London in Baker Street.'

'As does Dr Watson,' said Watson thinking he might help Holmes.

Holmes slapped himself. 'Idiot, ich bin dumm.'

She turned to leave but stopped. 'Mind you, sir, I don't think Sir Arthur would ever hire Mrs Hudson to work for him.'

The visitors came alive. 'Oh, and why is that?' asked Holmes.

Mrs Turner paused then spoke in a soft voice. 'The walls have ears around here.' The men nodded. 'Sir Arthur does not care for Sherlock Holmes or Dr Wilson or Mrs Hudson.'

Watson fumed. *Dr Wilson?* Holmes remained calm. 'Are you sure?'

'I once overheard Sir Arthur telling Major Wood he wanted to kill that damn detective.' She put a hand to her mouth. 'Oh, please forgive my language, sir. I normally never speak like so.'

'I didn't hear a thing.' He turned to Watson. 'What about you, Schmidt? Did you hear this enchanting lady say anything?'

'Not a word,' said Watson trying to sound German but getting his guttural technique wrong and sounding like a boyo from the valleys.

The housekeeper turned to leave. 'I'll pop back for the tea things later, gentlemen,' she said and left.

'Interesting,' said Holmes, 'sehr interessant.'

'Did I hear the woman mention a Dr Wilson?'

Not wanting to depress, or rather further depress his friend, Holmes lied. 'Jabez Wilson from *The Red-Headed League*.' Holmes resumed searching. 'Press on, old man,' he said, 'press on.'

They ignored the tea and tackled their task.

A few yards away, Major Wood picked up the telephone. After observing Sir Arthur for the last few days, seeing how he reacted to the manuscript, to Greenhough Smith and to Mrs Hudson, and having Lady Conan Doyle explain the fire, he decided to act. Help was needed—now. Wood made a telephone call.

'Good morning,' said J. M. Barrie, the author of *Peter Pan* and many other books and plays.

'Good morning, Sir James, it's Major Wood from Windlesham.'

'Woodie, how are you? How is the famous writer?'

The men made small talk until Wood cut to the chase.

'I am seriously worried about our friend, James. Something extraordinary has happened and Arthur has not handled it well.'

Barrie's enthusiasm pushed him to ask questions and discover how he might help his cricketing chum, friend and fellow writer. Wood explained the Hudson manuscript and its criticism of Doyle's writing.

'Sounds like a storm in a teacup, Woodie,' said Barrie. 'Doyle's grasp of spelling and grammar was terrible at best. It took him ages to master capital letters. Have you read his early material? The man is allergic to punctuation.'

'I'm afraid it's much more than typographical errors, James.'

'Well it's the publisher's job to edit manuscripts; nothing to do with the author.'

'The publisher's been here and is pressing Arthur to help promote the manuscript by this woman calling herself Mrs Hudson. Arthur is dead set against it and the whole business is getting out of hand.'

'Mrs Hudson, you say? Surely that's a pathetic nom de plume.'

'Of course it is but it adds salt to the wounds of our friend. I tell you, he's in a bad way.'

'But why would this woman, this writer make a fuss now? The stories are best sellers around the globe.' Barrie made light of the matter. 'Besides, Sherlock Holmes wouldn't give a fig for this type of nonsense.'

'Because this Mrs Hudson woman is proving difficult to find.'

Barrie hesitated. 'What? You mean she's vanished?'

'She came here, met Arthur, left her manuscript and disappeared.'

Barrie almost whispered. 'Are you saying she's been murdered?'

'I have no idea, James. But ever since she and her manuscript arrived, Arthur's been in a funk. His health is under serious threat.'

Barrie worried. 'Please don't think I doubt your diagnosis, Woodie, but surely an unheard of, nit-picking critic can never damage the great reputation of the world-famous Sir Arthur Conan Doyle.'

This prompted a silent pause before Barrie spoke.

'Hello? Major, are you still there?'

Wood whispered with a sense of anxiety in his voice. 'Last night he tried to destroy her manuscript.'

Barrie recoiled in shock. 'Destroy it! I don't believe you. How?'

'Around midnight, Jean saw a fire in the back garden. She ran out and Arthur hurriedly extinguished the flames claiming the fire formed a test for an incident in a new novel.'

Barrie became anxious. 'What new novel? I know nothing of this.'

'There *is* no new novel. Sir Arthur's pathetic explanation covered his terrible behavior.'

'My God, this *is* serious.'

'Jean doubted his story and this morning discovered a partly burnt page in the ashes.'

'And?'

'It's the remains of the frontispiece of the manuscript.'

'But that's preposterous. Arthur would never even consider destroying somebody's property and certainly not a fellow writer's. He's a quintessential English gentleman.'

Wood felt tempted to point out Sir Arthur was no more English than Barrie with both being born north of the Tweed.

'I tell you this in the strictest confidence, James. If Arthur learns of this conversation, I fear his unusual behavior may well escalate into something far more frightening. His shame would be unbearable.'

Barrie tried to make light of the serious matter. 'Come, come Woodie, you exaggerate, surely.'

'I only wish I did.'

Barrie's brain sparked. 'I know. I shall revive the Allahakbarries cricket team and make him captain. That'll cheer him up.' Wood showed little enthusiasm.

'Thank you, James,' he said in a monotone, 'but I fear padding up will do nothing to stop this downward spiral.'

Barrie now knew the seriousness of the situation. 'Here's a thought. Is he still active in the *Crimes Club?*'

'He is when not travelling.'

'Well why not ask one of his fellow members to investigate this manuscript and its missing author?' Wood perked up. 'They could do so on the quiet. There are chaps there who were spies or amateur detectives. I'm sure they'd love to help Arthur in his time of need.'

Wood perked up even more. 'An excellent suggestion, James,' he said. 'I'll get onto it straight away.'

'I take it he's not at home.'

Wood explained Sir Arthur's absence then mentioned how disappointed he was to miss the visiting German Professor whose praise for Arthur's historical novels gave Arthur immense pleasure.

'Professor Roth is a typical academic with his immaculate clothing, moustache and monocle. He's studying Arthur's research notes in the library as we speak.'

Barrie laughed. 'Are you sure Arthur didn't invite the man?'

Wood stalled. 'Invite the man? Well, yes he did, but only after the Professor approached Arthur.'

'Can you see a pattern developing?'

'I'm sorry, James. What are you talking about?'

'The character takes over the story.'

Wood fell into deeper confusion. 'What character?'

'Your academic sounds like Sherlock Holmes in disguise.'

A stunned Wood took a few seconds to absorb that statement. His mind refused to believe certain things. One, that Sherlock Holmes is a real person and two, that Sir Arthur would use one of his creations to bolster his, Sir Arthur's, failing historical novels' agenda.

'Well thank you for listening, James, and for your suggestions and offers of help. I'll keep you informed of Arthur's situation.'

'Thank you, Woodie and give my regards to Sherlock Holmes in the library.' He laughed with gusto which Wood failed to match.

The call ended and Wood pondered Barrie's so-called joke. *Is Sir James psychic? Like Sir Arthur, he shows a great interest in non-humans, fairies and the like. Does his experience with the wee folk grant him extraordinary powers? Was he guessing when he said the German Professor was Sherlock Holmes in disguise?*

Wood remembered Barrie's suggestion about fellow members of the *Crimes Club*. He wanted someone experienced in spying, who had something in common with Arthur and who would be totally discrete. If Sir Arthur discovered a colleague spying on his situation with the Mrs Hudson manuscript, the great man would be furious making his current state of despair even worse. Whatever happened, this proposed spy mission must remain hush hush.

Wood examined the list of members of the *Crimes Club* and one name leapt out at him. He found the correct telephone number.

Operation *Save Sir Arthur* began.

Chapter 17

INSPECTOR LESTRADE ADMIRED SHERLOCK HOLMES. *Liked* would be too strong a word and Holmes, despite his snappy comments about the policeman's abilities, allowed Lestrade to take the credit for some of the cases solved by the consulting detective. Now both men were preparing to farewell the investigation of crime.

When Lestrade first heard about Mrs Hudson's disappearance, he immediately wanted to help. He knew her well as the dear lady who opened the door at 221B Baker Street whenever the Inspector called to see Mr Holmes and Dr Watson. There she stood, always with a smile and a kind word.

Holmes saved Lestrade's reputation several times during their years together so "Bulldog" Lestrade wanted to return the favour.

He walked along Baker Street and knocked on the door he'd entered, oh, countless times before. He wanted to offer his services and those of Scotland Yard to help his "colleague" Mr Holmes. Lestrade composed a little speech.

"Do not worry, Mr Holmes. I feel sure Mrs Hudson is somewhere safe and we will find her and bring her home to you and Dr Watson. Please accept my word as a detective of longstanding; Mrs Hudson will be found."

Lestrade took pleasure in the fact he had given Mr Holmes moments of happiness due to his dogged police work. *I'll give his spirits another boost*, he thought.

At the front door, he cleared his throat then knocked. He waited. He heard someone or something, the door opened and Inspector

Lestrade froze. His jaw dropped and his mouth remained in the fly-catching position.

'Good morning, Inspector Lestrade,' said the landlady. 'We haven't seen you for some time. I thought you had retired.'

Lestrade recovered enough to speak. 'Good morning, Mrs Hudson.'

'I'm afraid we have some bad news, sir. We have a missing person.'

Lestrade did not know the term "a parallel universe" but would now understand its meaning if such a term were explained to him.

'Missing person?' he managed to ask.

'Mr Holmes has disappeared.' She couldn't miss the look of shock and confusion on Lestrade's face. 'Won't you come in, Inspector?'

He did and followed the landlady to her small sitting-room. His long list of questions would have to wait.

'It's kind of you to call, Inspector,' she said. 'I've left a message for Dr Watson and I think my next port of call will be the police. Is it a coincidence you are here or do you have psychic powers? Mr Holmes often said you were one of Scotland Yard's finest.'

Eventually Lestrade made a contribution; a pretty tepid one. 'Mr Holmes is missing you say?'

'He's been acting strangely of late, and it's all my fault I'm afraid. But I never thought he would go off without telling me and then not return especially at this important time.'

'Important time?'

'He's leaving; should have left in fact.' Lestrade struggled. 'Are you working on a case with him at present?' She twigged. 'Of course, that's why you're here. Do forgive me.'

'Mrs Hudson, wait, please.' She saw his anxiety, or perhaps his confusion. 'Might we go back a little?'

'Of course. Go back where?'

'You said Mr Holmes has gone missing and it's all your fault. I'm afraid I don't understand the part about it being all your fault.'

'Oh that's simple.' She related pretty much all that took place in this residence and elsewhere over the last few days starting with the announcement of her claim to be an author. In the past, Inspector Lestrade interrupted the great detective if he disagreed with a Holmesian statement yet with Holmes' landlady he said nowt; not a dicky-bird. How could he? Mrs Hudson uttered facts to astonish with the wit and delivery of an accomplished actress. With her information and presentation, she bamboozled the officer.

When her performance ended, Lestrade eventually said, 'I see,' although what he saw was through a glass darkly.

She made tea during which time he ventured a few questions until it dawned on him, suddenly and with force. *I'm in her book!* His mind buzzed with a mixture of eagerness and trepidation. *Would the landlady remember my mistakes? Does she know her tenant's the clever chap while I'm Watson of the Yard? Where's the book now?*

Her response would have made a publisher's publicity agent proud. She proved to be a natural when it came to marketing. Inspector Lestrade oozed desire to get his hands on her book. "I'll buy one; what are you selling?"

'What can Scotland Yard do to help find Mr Holmes, Inspector?' asked Mrs Hudson, keen to find her tenant if only to have him help her tidy up the editing of her book.

'Oh, there are many things, Mrs Hudson. Already officers all over London are searching for ...' He stopped as his brain rushed to catch up with his words.

'Already Inspector?' asked a confused landlady. 'But when did you learn Mr Holmes first went missing? I thought *I* told you.'

She did tell him. *Ah, tricky,* thought Lestrade. He and his many colleagues were searching for Mrs Hudson who wasn't missing at all. They should have been searching for Sherlock Holmes. Oh dear.

'Tell me, madam, regarding this manuscript about Mr Holmes and the cases he solved in conjunction with Scotland Yard, did you say it is currently with the publisher of *The Strand Magazine?*'

'I did. Mr Greenhough Smith has faith in my manuscript and will publish it as soon as Mr Holmes returns, collects his many things and retires. So you can see it's most important we find Mr Holmes.'

Sometimes, perhaps *often,* Inspector Lestrade lacked expertise when working on the same case as Sherlock Holmes. Now, the consulting detective's landlady took over from Mr Holmes, and her thinking, observation and deduction matched, even outpaced her famous tenant, leaving Lestrade lost. He stood to leave.

'Thank you, Mrs Hudson. I will return to Scotland Yard and co-ordinate the search for Mr Holmes. It will assist, madam, if you would kindly remain here at 221B.'

'Of course,' she said.

'I will return with news the moment I have any.'

She followed him to the front door. 'You are most kind, Inspector. And if you could keep an eye out for Dr Watson as well, I will be most grateful.'

'Of course,' he said, doffed his hat and fled.

He ignored Scotland Yard. The news about Mrs Hudson being missing wasn't true. The news about Mr Holmes being missing was important but Lestrade showed little interest in the missing detective. Frankly, he didn't care. He cared only about his reputation in this new book.

The big news for him was the discovery of Mrs Hudson's tome. *I might be in it,* thought Lestrade as he headed for *The Strand*.

There the members of staff experienced bedlam. The boss's desperation affected and infected everyone. He posted newspaper advertisements, wrote to readers of his magazine who praised Sherlock Holmes, and then, most dramatically of all, contacted the police to help find the absent landlady and author.

Staff at *The Strand* trod on eggshells. The editor absented himself and any inkling he might suddenly appear produced fear one could touch.

Any news about the missing Mrs Hudson brought hope and relief, and whoever found Mrs H knew the promise from the editor consisted of promotion, longer lunch breaks and a bonus at Christmas, such to make your toes curl. As the editor crisscrossed London interviewing people who responded to his newspaper ads and letters about Mrs Hudson, Inspector Lestrade entered Reception.

Young Ernest Balfour greeted the visitor. 'Good morning, sir.'

'Good morning. Is Mr Greenhough Smith available?'

'I'm sorry, sir. He's away on business.'

'I understand you have the manuscript written by Mrs Hudson about her life with Mr Sherlock Holmes and Dr Watson.'

Ernest sprang from his chair, excited. He wanted to tell the visitor the truth when something in the back of his mind urged caution.

'May I ask the nature of your enquiry, sir?'

'I wish to peruse the manuscript.'

Ernest hated his job. *Who is this gentleman? How does he know about the manuscript? And where the hell is Mr Greenhough Smith?*

'May I ask how you know about this manuscript, sir, and what your interest in it might be?'

'How do I know it exists?' replied Lestrade, half surprised and half outraged. 'It is my business to know.'

'I'm afraid I don't follow, sir,' replied Ernest, none the wiser.

Lestrade got nowhere so played his trump card. 'Because Mrs Hudson herself told me about it.'

Ernest's heart changed gears. 'Mrs Hudson told you?'

'Indeed, less than one hour ago.'

'In person, face to face?'

'Yes, in person!' The inspector replied with his voice rising in volume as he spoke. The last four words exploded from his mouth. 'My interest in the manuscript is because *I am in it!*'

Ernest panicked. The other day he blew the opportunity to hold on to Mrs Hudson when she first came to *The Strand*. Boy did he have strips torn off him for that failure. And then he wrote her address as 221B Baker Street, an address which doesn't exist. So if this man, standing before him right now, has been speaking to Mrs Hudson only a few minutes ago, then he, Ernest Balfour of The Cottage, Fingrith Hall Lane, Blackmore, Essex, must kidnap this gent, nail his boots to the floor if necessary, do anything rather than let him leave without disclosing the exact whereabouts of the missing author. It was that important.

'Oh sir, if you could possibly tell me where Mrs Hudson is currently residing, I'm sure Mr Greenhough Smith would be delighted to show you the manuscript.' Ernest froze. He wanted to beg. He slipped into a state of panic and sought clarification. 'Did you say, sir, you are named in Mrs Hudson's book?'

Lestrade felt better. At last some progress was being made. 'I did although I'm disappointed you fail to recognize me, the leading Inspector from Scotland Yard.'

Ernest cringed. *What have I done now?* 'Forgive me, sir. You are Inspector ...'

'Lestrade,' snapped Lestrade. 'Confidant of Mr Sherlock Holmes and acquainted with his landlady, Mrs Roodenvojack Hudson.' As he stated her first name, he passed his hand across his mouth making the name unintelligible.

'You know her first name?' gasped Ernest.

'Of course. I know everything.'

'Could you spell that please, Inspector?'

'L e s t r a d e. Now can we get on.'

It was all too quick and complicated for the clerk.

'Of course,' said young Ernie hoping like hell he could obtain the magic address of Mrs Hudson and her first name. *What did he call her?* Alas, he didn't go about it the right way. In fact, he made things worse. 'Forgive me again, Inspector Lestrade, but I believe Mr Greenhough Smith and Sir Arthur Conan Doyle have the only copies of Mrs Hudson's manuscript.'

'And your point is?'

'I wonder how you would know you are in the manuscript without having seen it.'

'Do you not know your Sherlockian cases, young man?' Ernest cringed again. 'I thought this is where Dr Watson's reports were published.'

'They are, sir.'

'Then I suggest you read his accounts of *A Study in Scarlet, The Boscombe Valley Mystery, The Hound of the Baskervilles, The Disappearance of Lady Frances Carfax*, and many, many more. I appear in each and every one of those cases.' He glared at Ernest. 'Need I go on?'

Ernest turned obsequious. 'That will not be necessary, Inspector.'

'So, now may I see if Mrs Hudson has kindly mentioned me in her manuscript and if so, in what light I have been cast?'

Talk about being perched on the extremely sharp horns of a dilemma. Ernest suffered. If he allowed this chap to peruse the document Mr Greenhough Smith declared the most significant manuscript he could ever publish, and which Ernest had been charged to guard with his life, and if something unfortunate happened to said manuscript, Ernest's life would not be worth living. However, if this gent knows where Mrs Hudson, the famous, brilliant, new and much-in-demand scribe can be found, and her first name, then Ernest must, absolutely must secure that address. But only by showing the Inspector the manuscript could Ernest unlock Mrs Hudson's whereabouts.

Help me somebody.

The young man decided. He asked the Inspector to take a seat and went to the editor's office. He prayed it would be locked. Then he prayed it would be *unlocked*. It wasn't. Ernest returned to Reception.

'I'm terribly sorry, Inspector Lestrade, but the editor's office is locked. I'm sure, sir, if you were to return later today, Mr Greenhough Smith would be happy to grant you an interview.'

Lestrade grumbled with rage. 'I don't want a jolly interview. I want to see if I've been given due recognition. All those stories about Mr Holmes allowing me to take the credit when he solved the cases are greatly exaggerated. Do you understand?'

'I do, sir, I do indeed, and I'll make a note of it.' Lestrade walked to the door and Ernest remembered. 'Oh please, sir,' he begged. 'Can you tell me where you last spoke with Mrs Hudson?'

To Lestrade, this was a silly question, a waste of time. 'In her home of course, at 221B Baker Street.'

'So she's not missing?'

'She's not but Sherlock Holmes is.'

He closed the door with a bang leaving Ernest with a new bombshell to survive, and to ponder his imminent sacking.

Chapter 18

WATSON'S FRUSTRATION SOARED. He didn't like the fuss over Mrs Hudson's manuscript or its contents—obviously. He hated seeing his friend take the matter to heart and behave erratically. And finally, dressing up in a ridiculous costume and pretending to be a German chauffeur called Schmidt capped off his despair.

Not so Holmes who thrived on the exercise. Searching for clues drove the detective. Once work beckoned, boredom disappeared. Holmes was keen; Watson miserable.

For Holmes, the only disappointment in this present situation was the absence of the literary agent. Holmes adored deception in a face to face meeting. He thrived on the challenge of duping people with his many disguises, and wished Sir Arthur was at home. Still, here they were, on the trail of what, he wasn't sure, and if Holmes didn't know, you can bet Watson had no idea.

Then, out of the blue, the Eureka moment arrived. Holmes found gold. At first he went all quiet wanting to confirm it wasn't fool's gold. Like Watson, he didn't know exactly what he might find but would know if and when he found it. He found it. He couldn't hold back.

'Watson!' he cried and both men froze.

'Holmes, are you mad?' hissed Watson. 'Keep your voice down.'

'Mea culpa,' whispered Holmes, surprised at his fundamental error but thrilled with his discovery.

'And remember I'm Schmidt.'

Rarely did Holmes make mistakes and never one so elementary. The find must be significant; no, stupendous. It *was* stupendous.

The visitors paused wondering if Major Wood or the housekeeper heard the cry from Holmes.

If so, would they react? Wood heard the cry but found it indistinct. He ceased work. *Did I hear the word, Watson?* He walked to the library, tapping on the door. He felt uncomfortable interrupting the academic.

'Herein,' called a voice with a German accent.

Wood opened the door and saw his visitors seated at the table with a mass of documents before them.

'Do forgive me, Professor,' said Wood. 'Did you call?'

'Ah, Major, you have discovered my excitement, my cry of joy in my native tongue as I found Sir Arthur's notes for his theme on the goodness of mankind. I have always believed the underlying truth to be expressed in the eponymous characters of *Micah Clarke* and *Rodney Stone*. Now I have the proof found.' He held up a document, the wrong one as it happened. 'How I wish the great author could be here so I might congratulate him in person.'

'Quite,' said an embarrassed Wood. 'Well I'll leave you to get on.' He smiled and left. Holmes and Watson exchanged glances. Watson sighed with relief, Holmes grinned with delight. He snatched up the document which caused him to cry out and whispered.

'I have found it, Watson; proof your so-called literary agent is a shyster.' He waved the paper. 'Forget Mrs Hudson and her penny dreadful. *This* is the real story.'

'Holmes, I have not the foggiest idea what you're talking about.'

The detective paced the room, his mind on fire. 'I believe your agent is in cahoots with our dear landlady.'

'What?' Never was Watson so bewildered. 'Doyle and Mrs Hudson are working together? How? Doing what?'

'We wondered where she got her information. How does she know so much about your writing?'

'She read the cases.'

'And received tips from your agent.'

'No.'

'He went through your writing, noting your mistakes and passed the details to Mrs Hudson. He's the power behind the throne.'

'Good Lord,' said an incredulous Watson.

'Doyle has betrayed you from the beginning and here is the proof.' He tapped the document. 'You sent him your cases and he tried to manipulate them. Why?'

'What do you mean, manipulate?'

'He tried to change our names.'

'What? Why?'

'He gave us nom de plumes, Watson.'

'I don't believe you.'

'Did you ask him to change our names?'

'Of course not. Why would I do that?'

'Because you had a habit of changing things.'

Watson took offence. 'I did not.'

'Oh come on. You moved your bullet wound from Afghanistan to Pakistan. Look, he wanted me to become Sheridan Hope.'

Watson scoffed. 'Nonsense, you're making it up.'

Holmes showed Watson the page of Sir Arthur's notes. 'I was to be Sheridan Hope and you, Ormond Sacker.'

Watson thought he'd stumbled into a bad dream. 'Ormond Sacker?'

'So instead of Holmes and Watson, we're to be Hope and Sacker.'

'But why give us nom de plumes at all? We're not criminals.'

Holmes hesitated. He was here on a mission—to stop Mrs Hudson's manuscript. He pondered. Is there a link between the MS and Sir Arthur's plan to write Holmes and Watson out of *The Strand*?

Both investigators pondered. *Why did Sir Arthur want to change the names of two famous people? Holmes and Watson were baptized with those names. And why choose Hope and Sacker?*

Watson got inquisitive. 'Did Mrs Hudson have a nom de plume? Why us and not her? I mean is Hudson her real name? Is that why she never told us her first name?'

'I'm proud of you, Watson but can we clear up one thing? Did you ask Mrs Hudson to ask Doyle to hide our true names?'

The doctor's eyebrows peaked. 'Me?' he demanded. 'Why would I do such a nonsensical thing?'

Holmes understood. 'Thank you, my friend. I know you're a humble chap, and not wanting to glorify your name is typical of your steadfast character and humility.'

Confusion grabbed Watson. It strangled him when Holmes changed the subject.

'And I'm sure you witnessed the doppelganger in the room?'

Watson floundered—again. Until this whole incident with Mrs Hudson's book, Watson felt sad about the retirement of Sherlock Holmes. Now his sadness was replaced by desperation. *Please God, let him retire today*, became Watson's new and fervent prayer.

For decades the faithful companion tried valiantly to help his friend. So often he missed clues or gave his honest opinion only to find he missed the boat—embarrassingly so. And in this moment, in his agent's library, his life with Holmes seemed about to expire.

I love the man like a brother. I am in awe of his ability to solve mysteries. But so often I have no idea what on Earth he is talking about. What the hell is a doppelganger?

'Come now, Watson,' said Holmes. 'It's staring you in the face.'

Watson knew he wanted to scream. He didn't because it wasn't in his nature, he was working undercover, and he desperately wanted to end their working relationship on good terms.

'I'm sorry, Holmes. Your question leaves my speechless.'

'Major Wood,' said Holmes.

'What about him?'

'He's your doppelganger.'

Watson wanted to ask several questions, the first of which being "What's a doppelganger?"

'Steadfast, impeccable manners, polite, considerate; the man is you to a tee, Watson. You and he are two peas in a pod.'

'I fail to see the truth or relevance of your observation, Holmes. And how does that help us stop Mrs Hudson's manuscript being published? And, come to think of it, where is it?'

Holmes enjoyed the distraction of his observation. 'It would appear your literary agent and I have something in common.' Watson didn't understand and didn't care. Holmes explained. 'Both Conan Doyle and I have chosen reliable, down-to-earth Victorian gentlemen as our companion and friend. Doyle met you all those years ago, liked you, and so chose a companion who reminded him of you.'

Watson grunted which could have meant anything. His confusion settled like a pea-souper. He walked to the window and gazed into the garden. 'Where on Earth did she get the name Ormond Sacker?'

'It's not Mrs Hudson, it's Doyle, your trusted literary agent. He's the one trying to change our names. And here's something else.' He read from the document. 'He tried to call you Dr *James* H. Watson.'

James? Jim? Jimmy Watson?'

'And I have another brother—Sherrinford Holmes.'

'I don't believe you. You're making this up.'

He showed the document to Watson who read and responded. 'James and Sherrinford? But why?'

'That my friend is the mystery I intend to solve. But it shows how Doyle took control of your writing. Before they reached *The Strand*, Doyle got his hands on your stories and suggested changes.'

'Do you think Doyle deliberately put mistakes in my stories?'

'Anything is possible.'

'And Mrs Hudson? Where does she fit in this scheme?'

'That we are yet to discover. But now it's time for the diversion we discussed. Are you ready?'

Watson wanted to return to London, hating the role-playing as a criminal, spy or dim private detective. 'As I'll ever be,' he said.

'Good show. You distract the Major and I'll investigate. Good luck.'

Watson crept through the house, bumped into the housekeeper, sought directions and found himself in the driveway beside the car they hired. Once there he lifted the bonnet and hit the horn.

Major Wood arrived and Watson, or rather Schmidt went into some rigmarole about checking the engine before the journey home.

A few seconds after the horn sounded, Holmes left the library. With Wood outside, Holmes landed in Sir Arthur's office looking for Mrs Hudson's manuscript. He found it—he couldn't miss it—and noticed the missing frontispiece.

That's been ripped out, thought Holmes. *Very interesting.*

Chapter 19

'HELLO ALFIE, IS THAT YOU?' asked the worried caller.

'Speaking.'

'This is your namesake.'

'Who?'

'Your namesake, Army rank-sake and parent-status-sake.'

'Woodie! How lovely to hear from you. How are you, old chap?'

'I'm well and yourself?'

'Good as gold, and how is Sir Sherlock? He missed the last *Crimes Club* meeting.'

'Busy as ever. He's giving a lecture in Hastings today and his diary is full to overflowing.'

'So to what do I owe the pleasure of this telephone conversation?'

Wood paused. 'I need the services of a spy.'

Mason laughed. Alfred Edward Woodley Mason enjoyed a grand sense of humour. He once worked as an actor playing bit parts in Repertory Theatre, and copied his friend Arthur Conan Doyle by working on a trawler in seas both rough and treacherous. He copied his fellow soldier Major Alfred Herbert Wood, a.k.a. Woodie, serving in WW1 and also reaching the rank of Major and, like Wood, never married or sired children.

Mason wrote *The Four Feathers* and created the famous detective Inspector Hanaud with his sidekick, a retired banker. Mason's famous professional detective spoke with a French accent and might well have been the basis and inspiration for another popular fictional sleuth.

So A. E. W. Mason had plenty in common with both Conan Doyle and Woodie. They went back a long way. In Mason's case a very long way back as he became a demon fast bowler with a run-up to match. Decades ago, Doyle, Wood and Mason were all cricket mad fellows.

Mason wondered about this phone call, and what Wood meant about needing a spy. Wood explained.

'Our mutual friend is having a spot of bother, Alfie,' said Wood, 'and you are the ideal man to save the day.'

'You flatter and intrigue with a single sentence,' said Mason.

'It's as if Sir Sherlock has been sent four feathers and the poor chap has no idea how to prove he most definitely does not deserve them.'

Mason wanted more. 'All I need to know Woodie, is when and where we meet? I assume the great man is not aware of these things.'

'Is the Café Royal still an old haunt of yours?'

'My dear fellow, what a question,' sounded an offended Mason.

'Is tomorrow at one suitable?'

'I have already chosen my tie.'

'And yes, Alfie, this is a job for a spy, top secret and for your eyes only. The great man must never know of this phone call or of our meeting tomorrow. Have I made myself clear, Major?'

'You have indeed, Major; until the morrow.'

The call ended. Alfred Wood felt relieved and Alfred Mason excited. He once worked in naval and counter-intelligence in WW1. His spying ability mixed with his acting skills, saw him deceive German officers and destroy their communication system.

A. E. W. Mason, Mr Multi-Talented, had the experience to succeed but could this novelist, actor, playwright, soldier and spy locate Mrs Hudson and save the career and health of Sir Arthur?

As an aside, not many people knew Alfie Mason once declined a knighthood, using the reason of nil issue. Being childless, he deemed such an honour useless if not to advantage offspring. Alfie's chum, Arthur Conan Doyle, coincidentally also initially refused a knighthood. But thanks to Sir Arthur's dear Irish Ma'am, Sherlock accepted after she gave him the rounds of the kitchen.

'Arthur, to refuse is an insult to the King.' Arthur knelt.

Chapter 20

WATSON COMPLAINED ALL THE WAY. 'I'll never master this car driving, Holmes. The sooner we're back in London the better.'

'You're doing a splendid job, Watson. Pull over around the next bend, if you please. No one will see us in this tranquil countryside.'

Watson stopped the car with an abrupt halt beside a babbling brook in a rural setting of that green and pleasant land. Holmes whipped off his false goatee and moustache then sprang out to change his clothes; the German academic became the English gentleman.

Removal of Watson's disguise proved harder. He wouldn't be wearing those boots ever again. 'I can tell you that,' he grunted. Age took its toll on the former British Army doctor now sporting a fine example of a middle-age spread.

Standing in his undershirt and long underpants, Watson prepared to step into his regular trousers when around the corner came a trap containing the wife of a local farmer and her two teenage daughters. Instinctively Watson threw his trousers over his head remaining still as the females, complete with giggles and shrieks, clip-clopped by.

'Have they gone?' asked the muffled Watson when the sound of the trap was no more.

'Indeed,' said Holmes. 'But I would have thought you might have covered your undergarments, Watson, to save their blushes.'

'I would have thought, Holmes, females are more likely to recognize me from my face than from my unmentionables.'

They finished dressing, put their costumes and props in a suitcase, and set off for the Crowborough garage to return the car.

They left the suitcase with the stationmaster at the railway station and walked to the local pub.

Enjoying a drink, they sat and listened. Watson knew the train was not due for some time but would have preferred the waiting-room and anonymity at the station to the regulars in the public house.

His friend had other plans and made conversation with a local. Holmes used a middle-class accent and, having established a basic rapport, he cut to the chase.

'I heard there is a literary chap in these parts with an interest in Sherlock Holmes,' said Sherlock Holmes.

'Oh aye,' said the regular.

'Does he enjoy a glass with his fellows?'

'No he don't. Him bein' far too busy with his ghostly encounters.'

Watson's ears pricked. Holmes pressed. 'Ghosts you say?'

'Aye. 'E's got this cockeyed belief we can talk to our dead folk through them séance meetings.'

Holmes played it cool. 'I take it you don't share those beliefs.'

The regular scoffed. 'Ha! I'd believe in Sherlock Holmes before all them ghost stories.' Watson studied his friend who gave a wee smile. 'An' I don't believe in Mr Sherlock Bloody Holmes neither.' Watson wanted to laugh *and* cry.

Sir Arthur, Lady Conan Doyle and the children returned to Windlesham from Hastings. Major Wood came out to welcome them. The patriarch was weary from the 30 mile drive but anxious for news. He and Wood remained by the car while the housekeeper accompanied the others indoors.

'Well, tell me man. What happened? Did the Professor arrive?'

'He did, Arthur and stayed for a good hour or more.'

'Is that all; only an hour?'

Wood was troubled. He knew his employer desperately wanted approval by academia. This worried Wood. 'He studied your notes in the library and expressed his disappointment at your absence.'

'What else did he say?'

'Oh, you know, the usual sort of thing; how he was delighted to be here and have the chance to study your work first-hand.'

'And?'

Wood had news he didn't want to share with his friend so spoke about another matter. 'There was something unusual. I thought I heard him cry out at one stage—Hobson, Dobson or maybe Watson.'

'Watson?'

'I'm not sure. I went to the library and he seemed genuinely excited. He said he found proof that your theme on the goodness of mankind was found in *Micah Clarke* and *Rodney Stone.*'

Sir Arthur came alive and grabbed Wood's hands. 'He said that? Those exact words?'

Wood nodded. 'He did.'

Sir Arthur beamed as his body buzzed with relief and excitement. 'Oh Woodie, this is the breakthrough I have dreamed about for years. Finally my serious writing is being recognized for what it really is. All those sales of Sherlock Showoff Holmes, all that mass hysteria about those short stories full of schoolboy howlers; forget them. Let's concentrate on my historical novels. They are examples of high art, quality prose, literature to last for generations.'

Wood remained still throughout showing none of the joy expressed by Sir Arthur who was so happy he failed to notice Wood's lack of enthusiasm.

'What else, Woodie? When does he wish to return? Did you tell him I will make myself available for any of his future visits?'

'Nothing definite, Arthur but he was certainly disappointed to have missed meeting you in person.'

'Excellent, excellent. Did he come alone?'

'No, he brought his driver cum secretary, a Herr Schmidt. I thought I knew the chap from somewhere; he reminded me of someone.'

Sir Arthur came back down to Earth. 'And has there been anything more from Smith or that odd woman and her manuscript?'

'Nothing; all quiet on that front.'

'Where is her manuscript?'

'It's on your desk.'

Doyle panicked. '*On* my desk?'

'Yes, I saw it there a few moments ago.'

'Not in a drawer, out of sight?'

'No.'

'But anyone might have seen it, even the Professor. He didn't go into my study I hope. If he reads that manuscript, he may think less of my historical novels.'

Wood tried to calm the author. 'It's all right, Arthur. He loved your novels.'

'Was he ever alone?'

Wood hesitated. 'No, Arthur, he was in the library,' lied Wood who experienced a sinking feeling. He remembered the car horn sounding and rushing out to see what it was all about.

What happened when I left the Professor alone in the house?

'I must get on,' said Sir Arthur who went inside thinking about Professor Heinrich Roth. Wood thought about him too, and dreaded telling Sir Arthur the latest, terrible news.

Wood's procrastination would only make things worse. His excuse was that he wanted to share the whole scenario with Major Alf Mason, spy extraordinaire. If he could resolve the visiting academic issue and the Mrs Hudson disappearance mystery, maybe Sir Arthur's career and legacy could survive and thrive. Fingers crossed.

Clearing his desk at the end of a long day, Wood was interrupted by Lady Conan Doyle. Her hands were shaking.

'Woodie, I must speak with you,' she whispered. 'Arthur's upstairs.'

'Jean, what's happened?' asked Wood catching her anxiety.

'I'm seriously worried about him, Woodie. He's getting worse. People in the audience today told me he seemed distracted. That incident with the fire in the garden was the tip of the iceberg. Something's happened in the last few days and he's acting strangely. I've never seen him like this. What's going on?'

'A lot, I'm afraid' said Wood. He could see she wanted answers so explained the manuscript from the little old lady giving only the basics.

'But that's silly. The Sherlock Holmes' stories are so popular. Surely a few errors are neither here nor there.'

'I'm afraid there are more than a few errors.'

'But even so surely that's not enough to make him react as he has.'

'Not only are there many factual errors, there are events which are not logical or not explained and as you know, Arthur is particular about facts and logic. He spent ages researching his historical novels.'

Jean panicked, 'Oh no, Woodie; are the historical novels being questioned too? He talked non-stop about the visiting academic.'

'No, no, the criticism is only about Sherlock Holmes, but it sounds as if Arthur is being called a hypocrite.'

'What?' gasped Jean.

'He has publicly stated his dislike of detective stories where the reader is left asking questions because things are not fully explained. This woman, Mrs Hudson, in her manuscript points out how Arthur does exactly that.'

'I don't follow.'

'In *The Red-Headed League*, the criminal tunneled from the gullible shopkeeper's cellar into the bank next door. The massive job took some time but Arthur never told the reader what happened to the clay Clay dug?'

A confused Jean asked, 'Sorry, what is the clay clay dug?'

'The main criminal, John Clay, dug the soil, be it clay or whatever. But what happened to it?' Jean shrugged. 'Exactly, nobody knows because Arthur failed to explain. Then in *The Adventure of the Blue Carbuncle*, Arthur decides the man's dusty hat is like that because his wife doesn't love him. If she loved him, she'd brush his hat.'

'What's wrong with that?' asked Jean,

'The wife could be dead, in hospital, visiting her elderly mother in Aberdeen or any number of things, none of which proves she doesn't love her husband.' Wood gave more examples increasing Jean's worry.

'So this new book is a threat to Arthur?'

'It could be, but there's more. It also contains details of the private lives of Holmes and Watson, things which don't appear in the stories. Arthur of course claims it's nonsense, and the incidents never happened but instead, were invented by this woman calling herself Mrs Hudson.'

'Can she do that?'

'Call herself Mrs Hudson?'

'And write things which aren't true?'

Wood shrugged. 'This new copyright law may restrict her but Greenhough Smith loves her manuscript and is desperate to publish; another reason why Arthur is in such a funk. He hates the manuscript while his publisher adores it.'

'I had no idea.'

'Greenhough Smith told Arthur his stories can be republished with the errors removed and Arthur liked that idea. But he's torn. Would any author with a substantial and successful oeuvre, want their errors up in lights for all the world to see?'

Jean looked shocked. Wood took her arm as she appeared ready to collapse.

'Thank you, Woodie, I'm okay.' She recovered. 'Is that all?'

Wood shook his head. 'There's more pressure from Greenhough Smith because he believes Mrs Hudson's book will be a bestseller with Arthur earning a share of the royalties.'

'But he didn't write the book.'

'Again it's to do with these new copyright laws.'

Jean's confusion doubled. 'So this is why Arthur is behaving so strangely?'

Wood nodded. 'As you well know, Jean, he wants to be accepted as the St Paul of Spiritualism. If he's made fun of or becomes a laughing-stock, his ability to go on speaking tours, promote séances, and help others contact those who have passed over, may be weakened.'

'You mean ruined,' added Jean.

Wood's glum expression said it all. He nodded and paused before he went for the jugular. 'I'm afraid it's really serious, Jean.' His expression frightened her. 'This is the greatest challenge Arthur has ever faced.'

Jean took control. 'Woodie, the solution is simple. Something must be done about the manuscript. Who is this Mrs Hudson?'

'And that's another problem; we don't know; nobody knows. We don't know her first name, where she lives, anything; and now she appears to have disappeared.'

'Surely people won't believe this Mrs Hudson is the landlady of Sherlock Holmes?'

Wood shrugged. 'Who knows? There are many readers who believe Sherlock Holmes, Dr Watson and Mrs Hudson are real people. If this manuscript is published, I think Greenhough Smith is right; it will be hugely popular.'

'But at least there is one ray of sunshine. Arthur is over the moon now this German Professor has shown an interest in his historical novels. We must do everything to help Arthur build a relationship with this man.'

Wood paused. He didn't respond and Jean's expression turned to horror.

'We can't,' said Wood in a whisper.

'Can't? Oh Woodie don't tell me he dismissed Arthur's historical novels. The Professor may be the only way we can save our beloved Arthur.'

Wood paused then delivered the news. 'His opinion about the historical novels doesn't matter because the man doesn't matter.'

'What?' gasped Jean, ready to collapse. 'He's a fake, Jean, a fraud.'

The colour drained from Jean's face and Woodie guided her into a chair. 'Tell me,' she whispered.

'I made some enquiries. There is no English Literature faculty at Leipzig University, and worse, no-one has even heard of a Professor Heinrich Roth.'

'Well who is he? Why did he come here?'

'I don't know but I have a plan to find out.' She waited for an explanation. 'I'll know more after a meeting in London tomorrow. But whatever you do, Jean, don't breathe a word to Arthur.'

Chapter 21

THE CAFÉ ROYAL in Regent Street has welcomed its fair share of celebrities over many decades. Oscar Wilde frequented the restaurant, and when A. E. W. Mason was a struggling actor and beginner novelist in Victorian London, the famous and wealthy Irishman took young Mason under his wing. Not that Alfie was on his uppers but Wilde could afford the fare at the Café Royal and proved just as generous with literary advice. How fortunate was Alfie to have such a mentor.

These two men later took different paths in life. Wilde to prison and ignominy and Mason to literary and military success. Today, decades later, Mason returned to the café Royal to meet his friend Alfred "Woodie" Wood. They were middle-aged bachelors, former cricketing chums and retired soldiers both with the rank of Major.

They sat and ate and drank and talked. The sumptuous surrounds of the establishment, its fine fare and outstanding wine list were of secondary concern. Wood had a tale to tell and Mason a role to play.

'I hardly know where to begin, Alfie,' said Wood. 'Some of the facts of the story are shaky at best, more like fantasy.'

With an impish grin, Mason pledged his commitment. 'I'm in, Woodie. I love an improbable mystery. Where do I sign?'

They smiled and Wood lowered his voice, unnecessary in the busy restaurant, preparing to tell the saga of Mrs Hudson's manuscript.

'But first I have a request to make, Alfie,' said Wood. The friends made strong eye contact. 'If I make what seems like a ridiculous statement, even more than one, please do not immediately dismiss it out of hand.'

Mason could see Wood meant business and replied in kind.

'I'm here to help our mutual friend, nothing more or less.'

Mason made the perfect spy by saying little and waiting until all details were revealed. When they were, only then did he begin to ask questions.

'Who else is working on this mystery? Am I the only investigator?' Perhaps only a professional novelist writing crime fiction or a former spy with a counter-intelligence background would ask such a question. Mason became both and skilled to boot. Wood knew he'd chosen the right member of the *Crimes Club* to save their friend.

Wood answered. 'I know one investigator is Herbert Greenhough Smith, the editor of *The Strand Magazine*. He's the driving force behind the manuscript being published. He's desperate to find this Mrs Hudson.'

'You keep saying *this* or *my* or *our* Mrs Hudson. Why?'

Wood hesitated. 'Can we discuss that later?'

Mason nodded. 'So there's only one person investigating the case?'

Wood grimaced. 'Not quite. I'm working on it, and Greenhough Smith, and you now, of course. And I've heard the Metropolitan Police are involved because someone reported this Mrs Hudson woman as a missing person.'

'Who reported her?'

'Greenhough Smith.'

'Okay, let's start with Mrs Hudson. You met her, Arthur met her, who else?'

'Greenhough Smith.'

'Describe her.' Wood hesitated. 'Pretend you're a novelist, Woodie, like your boss. Start with her age, size, clothing and mannerisms.'

'She's about 70, average height and weight. She dressed sensibly but not with extravagance, and spoke well.'

'Is she an educated woman?'

'Well if she wrote the manuscript, I guess she would have to be.'

Mason nodded. 'Good so far. That's what we *do* know; now tell me what we *don't* know.'

'We don't know her full name or address. Or rather we know the address she gave doesn't exist.'

Which was?'

'221B Baker Street.'

'Okay,' said Mason enjoying the preliminary chat thus far. 'We know it's a fictional address Arthur invented which makes Mrs No-First-Name Hudson forgetful or deceptive. She either can't remember her address or she doesn't want anyone to find her so she's given a fictional address. Which is it and why would she do that?'

Wood shook his head. 'Now you can see why I asked for your help.'

Mason grinned. He enjoyed being back on a case even if little old ladies with handbags at twenty paces were hardly a match for German spies in war time. 'What else?'

'And she's gone missing,' added Wood.

'And she's gone missing,' noted Mason.

Wood sniffed. He'd finished less than half his Dover sole 'There is another possibility.' Mason waited. 'She's the real Mrs Hudson who has now gone into hiding.'

Mason hesitated. He remembered Wood's earlier statement. "If I make what seems a ridiculous statement, please do not immediately dismiss it out of hand".

'Okay,' replied Mason. 'Let's leave that possibility to one side for the moment. Who else should we consider in this saga?'

Wood's cheeks puffed. This mystery seemed ideal for the great consulting detective, Sherlock Holmes. 'There are other people I met who may be involved.'

'Go on.'

'Yesterday, when Arthur was in Hastings giving a lecture, a German, a Professor of English Literature and his assistant came to Windlesham. Herr Roth asked for an appointment so he could research Arthur's notes on his historical novels.'

'And why are you telling me this?'

More hesitation from Wood who didn't want to make a fool of himself, or a bigger fool. 'I've since discovered the Professor is a fake.'

'Ah,' said Mason, 'the plot thickens. And you have no idea who this fraudster is?'

'No,' said Wood without conviction.

'But you have a theory. Come on, Woodie, out with it. I need every idea, thought and even your guesses if I'm going to get to the bottom of this. Who do you think this mysterious academic is and why the visit to Windlesham?'

Wood studied his friend who continued tucking in to his repast. 'Sherlock Holmes,' said Wood, and Mason's chewing froze. He recovered and resumed chewing.

Mason swallowed his food. 'Interesting,' said the former spy.

'You did ask, Alfie.'

'And why would Sherlock Holmes call on his creator?'

'To try and stop Mrs Hudson's manuscript being published.'

Mason chewed and nodded. 'And why would he do that?'

'Because it lists a number of the consulting detective's faults.'

Mason tried a summary of events to date. 'So the missing author is called Mrs Hudson, the name of the landlady in the stories about Sherlock Holmes, and her manuscript, or what we believe to be her manuscript, is in Sir Arthur's home, and a fraudulent Professor drops in to study the historical novels penned by our friend, and you suspect he is Mrs Hudson's tenant, the famous but fictional Sherlock Holmes?'

Wood preserved. 'He came with a driver who, I found frightening.'

'Frightening?'

'Yes, he looked and behaved a lot like me. The driver answered to Herr Schmidt, and yet I think I heard him being called Watson.'

'You think?'

Wood hesitated. 'Everything seemed … mysterious.'

Mason played cricket with Wood and Conan Doyle. The three men shared interests and careers and admired, trusted and respected one another. But now, Mason reckoned something unusual was afoot. He played it cool. He gave Wood no indication of the thought that Alfred Mason thought Alfred Wood might not be the full quid.

Mason knew many people accepted Sherlock Holmes as a real person or pretended to. He wasn't sure how many of these readers were serious or simply playing a game. Playing *the* game as it would come to be known.

'Tell me Woodie, have you discussed this situation with anyone, with Arthur?'

'I most definitely have not discussed any of this with Arthur. With his wife, Jean, yes but not using the same ideas I've shared with you. Oh, and I did have a chat with Sir James Barrie.'

'Ah, Sir James,' said Mason. 'And how is Peter Pan these days?'

Wood sounded serious. 'Peter Pan had a theory on the identity of the German Professor.'

'Not Captain Hook I hope.'

'James reckoned the German Professor was Sherlock Holmes.'

Mason took a deep breath. This "job" moved into the more-serious-than-he-first-thought category heading towards decidedly weird. 'Okay, and what do you think caused Sir James to reach that conclusion?'

'We were on the phone. I described the Professor, his appearance, clothing, speech, mannerisms and such, and straightaway Sir James remarked the man appeared to be like Sherlock Holmes. His words were, "Your academic sounds like Sherlock Holmes in disguise".'

The conversation lagged and both men ate in silence. Finally Mason pushed his plate aside, wiped his mouth and cut to the chase.

'Woodie, what exactly do you want me do?'

Wood thought long and hard. He opted for one simple task. 'Find this Mrs Hudson.'

'That's all?'

Wood nodded. 'And help me stop losing my mind.'

Mason leant forward and squeezed Wood's arm. 'Chin up, old man. We'll have this sorted before you can say Sherlock Holmes.'

Chapter 22

WATSON MOPED ON THE TRAIN back to London. He was still moping when he and Holmes returned to Baker Street. They avoided Mrs Hudson and she them.

'I hated everything, Holmes. You know I can't drive. Why couldn't you do the driving or find a cab driver?'

'I think once you drew the chauffeur short straw, Watson, it really had to be you.'

'And that uniform. The trousers were too tight and the jacket too big.'

'The cap looked impressive.'

'And those boots took an age to put on and two ages to take off. And don't get me started on that incident when those ladies—and two of them were young and impressionable—saw me in a state of undress. I have never been so humiliated.'

'Come now, Watson, you exaggerate.'

'Holmes, I might have been arrested for indecency on a public thoroughfare. Imagine the appalling publicity.' He acted as if reading a headline. 'Respectable doctor charged with lewd behavior.'

Holmes smiled. 'I thought you behaved with the utmost dignity, Watson.'

'And if all that wasn't bad enough, the outrageous attempt to change my name has made this the worst day of my life.'

'Watson, calm yourself.'

'What a sneaky ploy, a secretive smear, and designed to do what, I ask?' Holmes went to answer but Watson kept complaining. 'And of all the nom de plumes I could have been given, that wretched man chose Ormond. I mean, what's wrong with Fraser, Gregor, Callum, Rory or even Rabbie? Who would call their son Ormond? It sounds like the name of an obscure railway halt in the Highlands.'

Holmes allowed his friend to let off steam before gently guiding him back to civilization. 'The name change is irrelevant, Watson.

'Yes, but Dr Sacker? I mean Dr Wilson or Dr Motson or even Dr Flotsam are at least close, but Dr Sacker?'

'I should stop this, Watson. It's not the important issue we face, and besides, you do have an imperfect history when it comes to your name.'

Watson stopped. As so often happened, his friend said something to perplex the GP. 'I have no idea what you're talking about, Holmes.'

'Your wife, Watson—can't remember which one—once called you James. I would have thought John is reasonably easy to remember.'

Watson scrunched his nose. As usual, Holmes was right. The good doctor gave up on his proposed name change complaint.

'So tell me, Holmes, what happened when I created a diversion with you alone in the library?'

'I paid a visit to your agent's study where I made a significant discovery.'

'And?'

'I saw Mrs Hudson's original manuscript missing its frontispiece.'

'So she did deliver it to Sussex.'

'Someone did. The frontispiece had been removed with force and as to why, and where said page is now, I have no idea; destroyed I should imagine.'

'Pity the entire manuscript wasn't destroyed. So what's next?'

Holmes appeared rattled. 'I'm unsure.'

Watson frowned at the lack of a plan. The great detective remained all at sea. Mrs Hudson remained well ahead and cruising.

'Well we must do *some*thing, Holmes.'

'Indeed but until a plan appears, I will continue packing as my retirement is already overdue.'

'May I give you a hand? Many hands make light work, as they say.'

Holmes refused. He didn't want to leave Baker Street without stopping Mrs Hudson's manuscript. If he finished packing, he had no excuse to remain in London. With Holmes gone, Mrs Hudson could, would publish.

'You look worried, Holmes. This is not like you. What's wrong?'

Holmes paused. He had great respect for Watson and Mrs Hudson and found it hard to say what he was about to say.

'Mrs Hudson lied.'

'What?' Watson stared at Holmes.

'In this room she looked me in the eye and said, "I cannot visit the editor until you have officially retired". I haven't retired, officially or unofficially, and yet she has been to visit not only an editor but a literary agent too. She lied.' Watson felt fear. This sounded nasty. 'So desperate is she to publish, Watson, Mrs Hudson broke her word.'

A scary silence settled in the room. Both men were speechless. A major threat remained. The problem-solver confessed to having no leads, clues or solutions. Their situation had disaster and unhappy ending written all over it. Then it happened.

The unusual sound made both men gasp.

At *The Strand*, Herbert read the many replies to his ads and letters. Still they arrived and still the result was the same—no Mrs Hudson. Herbert despaired because Sir Arthur declined to support the book. Enquiries by the police produced nothing. And with Mrs Hudson missing, the manuscript could not be published without a contract signed by the author. No news was bad news. No-one knew Mrs Hudson's whereabouts.

Young Ernest knocked on the editor's door. 'Excuse me Mr Greenhough Smith, but the policeman who called when you were out has returned and wants to see Mrs Hudson's manuscript.'

Herbert groaned. 'Very well, show him in.'

A minute later, Inspector Lestrade appeared and the editor instantly recognised the officer from the police station last night. Lestrade's fervent desire to promote his legacy and re-write history meant he failed to recognise Herbert.

'Ah Inspector, have you come to tell me Mrs Hudson is found?'

'What? She was never missing.'

Herbert's jaw dropped. 'I beg your pardon?'

'She was never missing. It's Mr Holmes who's disappeared.'

Herbert wanted to cry. He failed sorting fact from fantasy but before he could attempt to pin down Mrs Hudson's whereabouts, Inspector Lestrade launched his tirade.

'Now sir, I assume your clerk has told you why I'm here.'

Herbert nodded. 'He has, but may I ask why you wish to examine the manuscript, Inspector?'

'It's libel, sir, plain and simple.'

Herbert didn't know what to expect but it certainly wasn't that. *Libel? What libel?* 'Did I hear you correctly, sir? You believe Mrs Hudson's work contains material which may be libellous?'

'I do but I can only be certain once I have examined the text.'

'I see,' said Herbert beginning to wish he'd never heard of Mrs Hudson or her precious publication—unpublished though it was. 'And may I further ask, Inspector, how does this alleged libel involve you?'

The detective scowled. He leant forward, tapped on the editor's substantial desk and spoke sotto voce. 'Because I'm in the manuscript, my good man. I am *the* Inspector Lestrade.'

Herbert's misery engulfed him as each new chapter in the Mrs Hudson saga became way too hard. Fortunately, some things were simple.

He knew Sir Arthur created a fictional character, the landlady Mrs Hudson. He knew a woman calling herself Mrs Hudson once sat in his office right where Inspector Lestrade sat now.

He knew there was, *is* an Inspector Lestrade in several of the stories created by Sherlock Holmes. Wait, no! Created by Arthur Conan Doyle and starring Sherlock Holmes.

But is there a real police officer, an Inspector called Lestrade? Little wonder Herbert wanted to go home.

'May I see the manuscript, sir?' asked an impatient Lestrade. 'I simply need to check I have not been maligned.'

'Maligned?' whispered a battered editor.

'Several times Mr Holmes allowed me to take credit for solving a case when he was the brains behind the arrest. Of course I've always disputed the claim, and now I demand to have it corrected in this new publication.'

Herbert searched for the copy of Mrs Hudson's manuscript wanting the visitor to leave and never return. He found it. 'Here it is.'

Lestrade grabbed the document, sat, used the editor's desk and searched for the names of particular cases. He turned pages muttering as he went. 'Mistakes ... errors ... what's all this about?' He found something. 'Ah, this one, yes this was my case.' He read further becoming frustrated. Annoyed, he glared at Herbert. 'I'm not in here. There's no mention of my name!'

'Well that's what Mrs Hudson has written, Inspector.'

'She can't leave me out. It's not fair.'

'Fairness is not always a quality found in biography, sir.'

'It's outrageous. I'll take action.'

This was getting out of hand. 'Wait, please wait!' cried Herbert, so loud his staff down the corridor exchanged worried glances. 'You want to take action for libel at being misrepresented, and now you want to take action for not being mentioned?'

Lestrade twitched. His distress matched Herbert's depression. 'It's not fair,' is all he said.

'Well make up your mind, man.'

Lestrade waved the manuscript. 'Is this all there is?'

'Yes, it's the only copy.'

'*Copy?* This is a *copy?*'

'It is. My staff dictated and typed it using the original.'

Lestrade found a new course of action. 'This is unacceptable. I must see the original.'

'It's the same as the copy, Inspector.'

'Every word is the same?'

Herbert hesitated. 'Yes.' His voice dropped, 'although the original does have notes in the margins.'

'Ah ha,' cried Lestrade in triumph. 'Kindly show me the original.'

'It's not here.'

'Well where is it? Mrs Hudson said it was here.'

Herbert nearly fell out of his chair. 'Mrs Hudson told you?'

'Yes. That's what I said.'

'In person?' cried Herbert, his volume performing a crescendo.

'Yes, in person,' replied Lestrade, matching the editor's volume.

'When?' demanded Herbert.

'When what? And don't shout at me.'

'I apologise,' said Herbert lowering his voice and trying to be calm. It was hard being normal. 'When, may I ask, did Mrs Hudson tell you about her manuscript?'

'About an hour ago. Last night a chap made a missing person report at Paddington Green Police Station.'

Poor Herbert cracked. 'That was me. *I'm* that person,' he snapped and pointed at himself. 'Look, it was me. Me!'

Lestrade remembered. 'Oh yes, I thought I'd seen you before.'

Herbert struggled to remain sane. Forget calm; sanity became his only goal—that and locating Mrs H.

Lestrade explained. 'I followed up the police report about Mrs Hudson being missing.'

'And?'

'She's not.'

'Not what?

'Missing. I've just come from having a nice chat with the woman.'

'Thank God,' whispered Herbert.

At last, at long last the mystery was solved. A real person, sitting in Herbert's office confirmed the sighting of another real person, the once missing Mrs Hudson who too once sat in that very same chair.

Herbert wanted details. 'Tell me, please, Inspector, where did you and Mrs Hudson have a chat?'

Lestrade felt better. He enjoyed being wanted and treated with respect. 'I popped in to 221B Baker Street and there she was.'

Herbert wanted to scream. The nightmare returned. 'No!' he cried. 'It can't be that address!'

Lestrade reacted to Herbert's distress. 'There now, sir, control yourself. She's okay. In fact Mrs Hudson was in rude health.'

'This is not happening,' bawled the editor.

'Hey, hey, hey,' said Lestrade seeking to pacify Herbert. It didn't work. Lestrade remembered. 'But wait! I've just remembered.' Herbert looked up, a glimmer of hope in his moist eyes. 'Mrs Hudson *is* at home but Mr *Holmes* is missing.' He pointed a finger at Herbert.

'Now there's a scoop for you. Get Dr Watson to write *The Adventure of the Vanishing Detective.*'

Herbert threw in the towel. Life no longer had meaning. 'I will,' mumbled the distraught editor, close to a breakdown.

'So where is the original manuscript?' Herbert couldn't think straight. 'Come on, man.'

'What?'

'Where is the original manuscript written by Mrs Hudson?'

'Ah, it's with Sir Arthur.'

'Sir Arthur? Sir Arthur who?'

Herbert couldn't take any more. He flipped. He stood and spat his words. 'Sir Arthur Conan Doyle, the man who invented you, although clearly with only a modicum of intelligence.' Herbert pointed at the Inspector. 'Now get out of my office before I call the *real* police.'

Such was the fierce expression, the occasional spittle, and vigorous arm movements displayed by Mr Greenhough Smith, Inspector Lestrade took off in alarm, followed haphazardly by the dribbling editor. Staff members stared in amazement at the never before seen histrionics from their beloved leader. True to form, Inspector Lestrade didn't understand the unsubtle insults hurled his way. He only wanted the original manuscript, apparently in the possession of this Arthur Conner Doyle chap, whoever he might be.

For Herbert, the search for Mrs Hudson continued.

Chapter 23

'DID YOU HEAR THAT?' asked a worried Watson. Holmes didn't reply but moved quickly to investigate. It was not the sort of sound one heard often, if at all, inside 221B Baker Street. Both men left the sitting-room and hurried towards the landing where horror awaited.

There on the stairs, Mrs Hudson's motionless body lay twisted and still.

'Mrs Hudson!' cried Holmes bending to help her. His shock and concern meant he barely felt the harsh rheumatic pain.

'Let me through, Holmes,' said Watson wanting to examine his former landlady. The stairs were wide enough for two people at a pinch. Now, with one seemingly lifeless body blocking the way, having even one older male trying to help, let alone two, made a tricky proposition impossible.

Pathetic, possibly tragic, best described the scene. Mrs Hudson tripped or slipped and fell head first from the landing. Being a lightweight and using her hands thrown instinctively to halt her journey, the poor woman lay on her front facing the ground floor with her face toward the banister.

'Try and remain still, Mrs Hudson,' said Watson assessing her condition. 'We'll have you moved as soon as possible.'

She whimpered. *Thank God, she's alive,* thought both men. She wanted to speak but the pain and shock kept her silent. 'Shall I call for an ambulance, Watson?' asked Holmes.

'One moment,' replied Watson. He addressed her. 'Is this painful, Mrs Hudson?'

Watson gently moved one of her arms causing a yelp of pain from the victim. Watson lifted his face and mouthed one word. Holmes disappeared.

Once a horse-drawn ambulance would have arrived but now London used petrol-driven vehicles. They were fitted to carry only one patient. The ambulance was one thing. The main issue was the challenge to raise Mrs Hudson from her painful and awkward position, carry her downstairs, and place her in the ambulance.

For the last week, Holmes and Watson constantly considered *that* manuscript. Not now. Now they constantly considered the survival of the person who created that manuscript.

Mind you its contents had given both men sleepless nights, Holmes in particular. He plotted to prevent publication. His disguise as Professor Roth gave him information he didn't yet know how to use. But whatever action he planned, he wanted to cause as little pain as possible to Mrs Hudson and his friend.

He remembered a case where he thought Watson might have been killed and so threatened his adversary. 'My God, sir, if you have killed Watson, you will never get out of this room alive.'

Now he wondered if the elderly woman who had been a huge part of his life was about to meet her Maker. Death dominated his thoughts. *There are more important things than my damn errors.*

Yet despite his friendship with Watson and undying respect for Mrs Hudson, subconsciously Holmes kept a spot in the back of his dolichocephalic head labelled, *Stop that manuscript.*

While they waited for the ambulance, Holmes and Watson never left Mrs Hudson's side. They encouraged and sympathized with her. She didn't, couldn't speak. Eventually the ambulance arrived and the tricky task of moving Mrs Hudson began. With difficulty and pain for the patient, she made it safely to the vehicle.

'Where will you take her?' asked Watson.

'St Mary's, sir,' said the driver.

'We'll follow,' said Holmes hailing a cab.

They waited at the hospital in a corridor near the entrance. Their genuine concern for Mrs Hudson meant both men were anxious and sad. Holmes remained his cool self although in his chest, the automaton's heart beat faster. Watson couldn't sit still. His medical experience told him if an elderly person suffered a serious fall, that fall could often be the beginning of the end.

The threat of her book, as surprising, stressful and worrying as it was, meant nothing now. The life of this woman, so kind and supportive, so much a part of the lives of these two middle-aged men, was clearly in the balance.

'What is the procedure in a case like this, Watson?' asked Holmes.

'She'll be assessed and the results will determine whether she requires surgery, some other form of treatment or simply rest.'

'And how long before we receive some news?'

'Come now, Holmes, a man of your infinite experience; every case is unique, every situation has its own rules and outcomes. I could just as easily say "your guess is as good as mine" and yes, I know, you never guess.'

Watson's reply impressed Holmes who gave an imperceptible nod, and paced the corridor. Not easy as staff came and went. An elderly woman supported by her adult children came from a room, weeping silently. Holmes and Watson exchanged glances.

The minutes ticked by and the hardest part of the waiting was not knowing. Holmes found his patience running low. A nurse came from a ward, busy on her rounds.

'Excuse me, Sister,' said Holmes, and Watson worried.

'I'm sorry, sir, I have an urgent task,' she said without stopping. She disappeared.

'I simply want some news, Watson, any news. A snippet would be fine, good or bad, and, of course, hopefully good.'

Watson stood. 'We could try the main reception area.'

'Good old, Watson,' said Holmes.

They headed along the corridor stepping aside to give way to staff pushing or helping patients en route to their next destination.

They reached the busy reception area with staff not having a moment to relax. The visitors stood back as their request seemed minor when others were clearly in need of immediate care.

Finally, with a lull in the hurly burly of hospital admissions, Holmes approached the desk where a thick-set, middle-aged woman appeared to be in charge.

'Yes?' she said without grace or favour.

'Good evening, madam,' said Holmes. 'We wish to enquire as to the wellbeing of a patient who has recently been admitted.'

Constance Cumberbatch ran the reception desk. Her shift was drawing to a close and she was keen to head home to Lewisham. She dealt with all sorts in her job and when a couple of toffs approached and referred to the "wellbeing of a patient", Connie failed to be impressed.

'Name?' she said, still without a scintilla of humanity.

'Hudson,' said Holmes.

'First name?' barked Cumberbatch.

Holmes hesitated and Watson butted in. 'Missus,' he said and Connie's sense of humour, already on its last legs, tottered.

'Gentlemen, this is a busy hospital with hundreds of patients. If you want me to find your wife, mother, daughter, sister or *mistress*— she added volume and a touch of cynicism to the last word—you'll need to give me *all* the details. Now what's her first name?'

'I'm afraid, madam, we cannot tell you,' said Holmes.

'Then I'm afraid, gentlemen, I cannot tell you Mrs What's-'er-name Hudson's *wellbeing*.' She resumed work on another task. Holmes and Watson exchanged glances and, for once, Watson took control.

'I do beg your pardon, madam,' he said. 'I'm a doctor and fully understand the need for complete and correct information.'

Constance sort of believed the man calling himself a doctor. 'I take it you've only just become acquainted with this woman which is why you don't know her first name.'

'Oh no,' replied Watson with Holmes wanting to silence his friend. 'We've known her for more than twenty years.' Holmes cringed.

Constance snarled. 'Twenty years and you don't know her first name?'

'She never told us and we never asked. Did we?' asked Watson turning to his friend. The expression on Holmes' face was worth painting.

'I think I've heard enough, gentlemen,' said Constance wanting the time-wasters to hop it quick smart. 'You're telling porkies.'

Watson fell into a state of confusion whereas Holmes with his working knowledge of East End slang knew exactly what she meant. He stepped forward.

'I assure you, madam, we do indeed know and care about Mrs Hudson as she was and, in my case, still *is* our landlady.'

Constance felt the pressure. A couple of the things these men said had a ring of truth about them. They didn't look like fraudsters and, if they were, what could they possibly hope to gain by enquiring about the "wellbeing" of a patient. But Constance didn't come down in the last shower and when in doubt, she always opted for disbelief.

'Your landlady is called Mrs Hudson?'

Watson came alive. 'Indeed,' he purred. Now they were getting somewhere. Constance killed his happiness.

'And I suppose you're Sherlock Holmes and Doctor Watson?'

Watson again hit the heights of joy but, like a comet that flashed across the heavens and vanished, so too did his ecstasy.

'Pull the other one,' said Constance who stood and walked away.

Holmes took Watson's arm. 'Come along old fellow. Let's return later.'

They headed for the exit and were almost there when a voice was raised. 'Dr Watson?' Holmes and Watson stopped and were joined by a middle-aged man.

'Yes, I am Dr Watson.'

'You don't remember me?' asked the man, a tad crestfallen but delighted to have spotted someone he knew. He turned to Holmes and smiled again, even brighter. 'And Mr Sherlock Holmes; how do you do, sir?'

Watson wore his usual blank look, and even Holmes racked his brain without success. Old age had its consequences. The man decided to jog some memories.

'Do you remember a dresser who worked for you at St Bart's, and a chance meeting at the Criterion Bar, and an introduction that started it all about twenty years ago?'

'Stamford,' exclaimed Watson with smiles and handshakes all round.

Holmes remembered, shook hands without emotion, and wanted to get on, whereas Watson and Stamford were up for a chat.

'Just think,' said Stamford, 'if I hadn't brought you two gents together we might never have heard of the famous detective and his friend.'

'The world has much to thank you for, Stamford,' said Watson. 'What say you, Holmes?'

'Indeed but can we get on?'

Stamford sensed their anxiety. 'Are you investigating a new case, Mr Holmes?'

'Yes, it involves a missing person.'

'Well if there's anything I can do to help,' said Stamford with undisguised enthusiasm, 'I'd count it a privilege, gentlemen to be able to help, even in some modest and minor way.'

Holmes wanted to kill the situation. 'We're trying to locate a friend who has been admitted to this hospital.'

Stamford had enthusiasm to burn. 'Oh well, say no more. I've been a porter here for years. What's his name?'

'*Her* name,' said Holmes, is Mrs Hudson.'

Stamford recoiled in horror. 'Not Mrs Hudson, the landlady at 221B Baker Street, the lady I introduced you to all those years ago?' Watson nodded. 'Oh how terrible. She must be elderly now. How is the dear old lady? Please tell me it's nothing serious.'

Holmes showed not an ounce of gratitude only impatience. 'We don't know her condition because we can't locate her.'

Stamford buzzed with excitement. It was a re-run of his brilliant introduction all those years ago. Holmes and Watson became famous with their brilliant crime-solving investigations—and it all happened thanks to Stamford. Now he delighted in his largely unknown role by being part of their latest case.

'This way, gentlemen; if you want someone found, I'm your man.'

'Good show, Stamford,' said Watson who looked at Holmes. His nod of approval got things moving.

They set off back inside the hospital, Stamford's stamping ground. He knew the shortcuts and the right people to ask. They made progress although Holmes' patience wore thin due to Watson stopping to greet former medical professionals he knew years ago.

'Come along, Watson,' muttered Holmes through gritted teeth.

Eventually they reached the right floor where Stamford found the doctor treating Mrs Hudson. Dr Mortimer was polite and helpful if a little absent-minded. Holmes observed a strand or two of brown dog hair on the cuffs on his trousers.

'Mrs Hudson is comfortable,' said Mortimer. 'She appears to have no broken bones but does have some nasty bruising. We have her pain under control but there is concern about her heart.'

That statement whacked Holmes and Watson hard in the face. Stamford too was upset. Broken bones they were expecting but a troublesome heart shocked all three.

Watson knew what to ask. 'Is it a weak heart, Doctor?'

He nodded. Holmes took control. 'Are we able to see her?'

'Not at the moment, but possibly tomorrow or the day after.'

'Are we able to give her a message?'

'Of course.'

Holmes spoke. 'Please tell her that Dr Watson and Mr Holmes wish her a speedy recovery, and she is not to worry as we will take care of 221B Baker Street until she returns.'

Watson worried about the "taking care of Baker Street" business, and the doctor nodded. 'I'll pass it on,' he said, admiring the relatively long structure of Holmes' head.

No-one spoke. What next? Holmes broke the ice.

'Is there anything else we should know?' asked Holmes.

Mortimer hesitated and all three men felt a tightening in their chests. 'There is and it's not good news.' The doctor paused. 'We are not sure when Mrs Hudson will be able to go home, if at all. You should prepare yourself gentlemen—you may need a new landlady.'

Chapter 24

THERE WAS NOTHING to gain by staying at the hospital. Stamford offered to keep an eye on their landlady and bring them any news. He was over the moon to have met up with two of his heroes.

Those heroes returned to Baker Street where Watson made an announcement. 'Holmes, I have decided to move back to Baker Street as a temporary measure.'

'Really, Watson, there's no need.'

'There is you know. I want ready access to the hospital in case Mrs Hudson ...' He looked at his friend.

'Of course,' said Holmes, 'perfectly understandable.'

'And I want to be here to keep an eye on you, my dear Holmes.'

Holmes bit his tongue. He wanted to tell Watson he didn't need a nanny but held back.

'Apart from Mrs Hudson's health, there is your packing, Holmes, and that minor matter of Mrs Hudson's manuscript.'

Holmes nodded, impressed by Watson's seldom seen wit. 'Everything is under control, Watson, everything.'

Watson grinned. 'It'll be just like old times, Holmes.'

'Nothing of the sort,' snorted the automaton. 'We'll have no receptionist, secretary or servant, and certainly no breakfast in the morning!'

'We'll survive, and let's hope dear Mrs Hudson does likewise.'

Next morning Watson enquired at the hospital and returned to Baker Street with news. Holmes continued packing at what could only be described as a lazy snail's pace.

'The doctors are pleased with her lack of broken bones, Holmes, but she has some badly bruised limbs and her weakened heart is always a concern. And as Dr Mortimer said, there is little chance she'll be coming home soon.'

Holmes displayed his blunt side. 'Will she ever come home?' Watson grimaced. 'Her age is such she may require constant care. And hopping up and down the stairs here at Baker Street would appear to be out of the question.'

Watson pondered the subject. 'The lady is a fighter, Holmes. Did you ever see her flinch or refuse a task in all the years you have lived here?'

Holmes could not recall one such occasion. 'Never.'

'Our motto in caring for her should be, "Take it one day at a time".'

'Is she in much pain?'

'Thankfully no, and of that we can be confident. I spoke to a nurse who told me Mrs Hudson's brain appears to have suffered no ill effects and she manages to communicate well with staff.'

'When should we pay her a visit?'

'I would leave it for a day or two. She will be glad to see us both. However, we need to rehearse our lines.'

'Lines?' Holmes rarely became curious about the sentences uttered by his friend. Now his ears pricked.

'In case you've forgotten, Holmes, you retired a week ago and are now living on the Sussex Downs. What will you say when Mrs Hudson enquires about your current address?'

'I have the perfect explanation, Watson. I could not bear to leave Mrs Hudson's abode empty and unloved. I am ready to leave tomorrow but will remain here as long as it helps Mrs Hudson.'

'It's so unlike you to lie, Holmes,' he said indicating the many still unpacked objects. 'You are certainly not ready to leave.'

'A mere trifle, Watson; I could be ready to leave in a few hours.'

They surveyed the state of the room and then one another. Watson changed the subject. 'Visiting hours are from 2 until 4.'

If things were messy at Baker Street, they were as bad if not worse in Crowborough where confusion ruled the Windelsham corridors. Sir

Arthur's reaction to the dreaded manuscript continued apace. He tried once to destroy it, thankfully unsuccessfully, and remembering his folly caused him more pain than its contents. He felt ashamed.

Honour and *honourable* were key words in the life of Sir Arthur Conan Doyle. Even thinking about destroying someone else's property was anathema to him and his conscience copped a battering.

His maudlin behaviour made others depressed. Major Wood suffered the most. His worries were multiplied because of the secret he discovered—Sir Arthur's ray of sunshine, Professor Roth, was a fraud whose unknown identity and motives ramped up the conflict.

Finding the strength to tell his friend the terrible news became Wood's greatest challenge. He watched as Arthur slipped deeper into depression. The writer clung to the hope that at last the world would salute his historical novels and label him as a true man of letters.

All his success with Sherlock Holmes amounted, in Sir Arthur's mind, to cash without credibility. His dream involved being named alongside Scott, Dickens and Thackeray. Thanks to the German academic, Sir Arthur reckoned his dream could become reality. Forget Mrs Hudson's manuscript. Forget his error-strewn detective tales. Literary respect, possibly immortality awaited the good doctor.

But no, it didn't and Wood couldn't bear to kill Sir Arthur's dream.

'You must tell him, Woodie,' said Jean when the two were alone.

'I will, Jean, but it has to be the right time.'

'There is never a right time to tell bad news. The longer you delay, the worse it becomes for everyone.'

Wood looked at Lady Conan Doyle. He nodded. 'You're right. I'll tell him now.' Wood headed for Sir Arthur's study. Jean followed. She would need to comfort her husband once he heard the terrible news.

As Wood approached the study, he thought he'd vomit, but stopped on a sixpence when someone rang the front door bell.

Sir Arthur called. 'I am not at home, Woodie. Is that clear?'

Wood stood in the open doorway. 'It might be the King, Arthur.'

'I said I am not at home, not even for His Majesty.'

Wood grimaced. He'd been saved by the bell but the pressure to come clean got harder and harsher. He headed for the front door.

Chapter 25

A. E. W. MASON fitted the job description perfectly. Writer of crime fiction, wartime spy working successfully in espionage and counter-espionage, member of the *Crimes Club*, express fast bowler and a damn fine chap to boot; indeed the perfect man for the job.

Alf Mason knew Arthur Conan Doyle, J. M. Barrie and Alfred Wood. He knew everyone. But Mason was more Wood than Doyle and Barrie, with his head screwed on the right way.

While Barrie and Doyle were keen on fairies and life after death either through spiritualism or Neverland, Mason was down-to-earth. Call him Mr Practical. Of course he understood the meaning of the expression, "the suspension of disbelief" but being grounded in reality, Mason would never be fooled into thinking Sherlock Holmes was anything other than a fictional character. Or would he?

If Mason wished to find Mrs Hudson—the one who visited *The Strand* and the home of Sir Arthur Conan Doyle—then find her he would. Mason had no time for hunting some fictional character who lived in a house that didn't exist, famous address or not.

Mason wanted to help his fellow Major, his pal Woodie, and his fellow fictional crime writer, Arthur Conan Doyle. But Alfie Mason didn't believe in the wee folk, Wendy or Sherlock's Mrs Hudson.

He headed to the office of *The Strand Magazine* and its editor, one Herbert Greenhough Smith.

In Reception, young Ernest Balfour met many eminent people. Writers both famous and "up and coming" entered this office. A. E. W. Mason enjoyed impressive credentials. His novel, *The Four Feathers*, attained great reviews and wonderful success. Filmmakers eyed it with eager anticipation. Mason's fictional Inspector Gabriel Hanaud and his sidekick, the former City of London financier, Julius Ricardo, won plaudits from readers with some writers being inspired to write their own crime fiction.

'Good morning sir,' said Ernest, rising to greet the celebrated author.

'Hello, young man,' said Mason handing Ernest his card. 'May I have a word with your famous editor?'

'Of course, sir, one moment please.' Ernest hurried from the front office. His enthusiasm infected the editor who naturally knew of the successful novelist with Greenhough Smith hurrying to greet Mr Mason. Soon both men were seated in Herbert's office. Both were excited although for different reasons.

The editor thought the author might have a manuscript for *The Strand Magazine*. The author thought the editor might have the clue to unlock the mystery of the mysterious and missing Mrs Hudson.

'I'll come straight to the point, Mr Greenhough Smith.'

'Please, sir, do call me Herbert.'

Mason smiled. 'Herbert, I need your support.'

Those words turned up the anticipation of a new publishing venture for Herbert and *The Strand*. Sadly, for the editor, Mason's next words would dash any high hopes.

'I want you to help me find the writer calling herself Mrs Hudson.'

You could almost hear the air escaping from Herbert's inflated tyre of dreams. 'Mrs Hudson?' he managed to squeak.

'My good friend, Major Alfred Wood has asked me to help him find the elderly lady who has written a manuscript highly critical of Sir Arthur's wonderful tales. Major Wood told me you are up to date with the situation and we all believe the sooner we find this woman the better. Do you agree, sir, and do I have your support?'

What could Herbert say? 'I do agree, and you have my support, sir.' The editor's flattened hopes hopped onto the rollercoaster and began heading up again. Herbert too wanted to find Mrs Hudson. Did he ever? And if the famous spy and novelist was on the hunt, this could be the answer. Mrs Hudson might soon be found, her contract signed, and the profits of *The Strand* would start to rise and rise.

'I believe she came to see you here at *The Strand*,' said Mason.

'Twice,' replied the editor.

'Twice!' said the former spy. 'Please, tell me what happened.'

Herbert ran through the Mrs Hudson crisis, how she left giving a false address and was now missing, how he'd placed advertisements and written to readers. Mason asked questions and received more details. He reckoned the editor behaved logically and sensibly. But everything changed when Herbert related his visit to the Paddington Green police station.

The editor's explanation of the response by the Sherlock-believing coppers quickly changed the mood. Mason, legally speaking, changed Herbert's status from that of a witness to that of a suspect. *The man is delusional.*

'I'm sorry, Herbert. Did you say the police asked for a photo of Mrs Hudson, and you provided a sketch by the man who illustrated many of the Sherlock Holmes' stories?'

'I know it sounds unusual, sir,' said Herbert, 'but the police were keen and I had the sketch.' He moved to a table. 'We've had posters printed.' He handed one to Mason.

The former spy couldn't help himself from saying the following. 'But the Mrs Hudson in the stories in *The Strand* is a fictional character. The woman who came not once but twice to your office was *is* a real person. The two cannot be the same, surely.'

Herbert spoke with a serious expression. 'I understand, sir, of course I do. But ever since I tackled this mystery, everywhere I go I meet people who are convinced the Mrs Hudson I met is the Mrs Hudson who lives at 221B Baker.'

Mason continued to struggle. The man sitting opposite him had substance—was a successful businessman, a man of letters and of high intelligence.

'But the address is fictitious, it doesn't exist,' argued Mason. 'Baker Street is a short street. I don't think it even goes up to 100. There is no 221A, B or any other letter. There is no 221.'

'I know, and that's the major stumbling block.' Mason regarded Herbert as the major stumbling block. 'Mrs Hudson sat in this office and gave us her address. We naturally checked it out and discovered, as you have rightly said, it doesn't exist.'

'Surely you must have known that already. How many Sherlockian stories have you published?'

'Almost the entire Canon and we hope for more from Sir Arthur.'

'Indeed, and if so, you must have known the Baker Street address is fictional.'

Herbert wrung his hands. He now resided in publishing purgatory. Mason pondered his own position and finally reckoned he could see a way out of the mess.

'So the obvious conclusion is that the Mrs Hudson, who gave you the manuscript, lives somewhere else and does not want her address to be known.'

'Obviously,' agreed Herbert. 'Or her name. Don't forget she chose not to give us her first name.'

'And you've placed newspaper advertisements and contacted readers of *The Strand* trying to find her, and the police, God knows why, have her listed a missing person?'

'All correct, sir, and it has got us exactly nowhere.'

Mason took a long breath. If this editor was his only source of facts to find this missing woman, then the task just became more difficult.

'Can you name anyone else who dealt with Mrs Hudson, the real one I mean, the one who came here to your office?'

'Sir Arthur Conan Doyle and his secretary, Major Wood.'

Mason nodded. He knew about those two. 'Anyone else?'

'Yes, a policeman.'

Mason's hopes rose although not in any spectacular way. 'A policeman you say?'

'Inspector Lestrade from Scotland Yard came to *The Strand* twice and the second time he acted in a very irate manner and spoke about suing for libel.'

This was too much for Mason. His mind flooded with unbelievable thoughts. *A real policeman came to The Strand with threats of legal action?* 'So you met this officer in person?'

'Here and at the Paddington Green police station when I went to make a Missing Person report.'

'And?' asked Mason, a feeling of dread rumbling within his soul.

'When he came here, he demanded to see Mrs Hudson's manuscript believing she may have continued the libel perpetuated by Sir Arthur in a number of the cases solved by Mr Sherlock Holmes.'

Mason rarely screamed—well he did as a child when he touched a hot stove—but now, in his later years, a scream gathered strength, desperate for release.

'I'm trying to understand the sequence of events, sir,' said Mason. 'Is there not an Inspector Lestrade in some of the Conan Doyle tales?'

'Yes sir, I just told you.'

'No you didn't. You told me you met a police officer with that name here and in a local police station.'

'At Paddington Green, sir.'

'And that officer subsequently came here complaining about the way his character is described in Sir Arthur's stories?'

'That's it in a nutshell, sir. I hope it helps.'

'I will think on that, Mr Greenhough Smith.' No more of this "Call me Herbert" business. Mason went to stand but thought of another question. 'What occurred at the end of your conversation with Inspector Lestrade here in this office?'

'He wanted the original version of Mrs Hudson's manuscript—I only have the copy—and I informed him the original is safely in Sir Arthur's keeping.'

'You sent Inspector Lestrade to Sir Arthur's home in Sussex?'

'I wouldn't say "sent", sir. If he did go, that would be his business.'

This time Mason did stand. 'Thank you for your time, Mr Greenhough Smith. You have provided me with some, shall I say, interesting information.'

Herbert walked his visitor to Reception. 'If ever you have a new work, Major Mason, *The Strand* would be delighted to assist with all your publishing needs.'

Mason and Herbert shook hands with the visitor glad to be outside in the fresh air. Mason became another who would have understood the "parallel universe" expression had it been available at the time.

He needed a stiff drink.

Chapter 26

WOODIE HEADED FOR THE FRONT DOOR. The knocking continued. He spied Jean en route and they exchanged looks. He paused and she whispered, 'You have to tell him, Woodie.' He gave the faintest of nods and reached the front door. In a way he hoped it *was* the King. Despite his snappy command, Arthur would be in awe if His Majesty called at Windlesham. Such a visit would lift the author from his current depression, from his Grimpen Mire.

It wasn't the King. A diminutive Scot, a wee Jock, one James Michael Barrie, *Sir* James, stood on the doorstep grinning.

'Hello Woodie. I was passing and, on a whim I said to myself, I must pop in and see how my old pal, Dr Doyle is getting on.' He winked and Wood understood.

'It's lovely to see you, James. Please, do come in.'

Lady Jean Conan Doyle floated in and kissed the visitor. 'Oh James, how lovely to see you.'

'I assume the Edinburgh boy is at home and receiving.'

The others went quiet. 'He's here, James,' said Wood, 'but in the depths over this damn manuscript.'

'Still?' asked Barrie.

Wood whispered. 'And he doesn't know about the German Professor being a fake.'

'Oh dear,' said Barrie seeing the pain on their faces. 'Well I'll say nothing of those matters and concentrate on getting the old boy up and about and smiling again.'

'You're an angel, James,' said Jean and took the man, who made the name Wendy popular, through the house and to her husband's study. Wood tagged along with fingers crossed and heart racing.

'Arthur,' called Jean as they approached the study.

'Go away,' he called. 'I've moved to South America.'

Sir James stood in the open doorway. Sir Arthur turned and saw his visitor. Doyle's face lit up. Here stood a true friend, a fellow Scot, a co-writer with a conscience and a spirit to help his fellow man.

The men embraced. Once, before Barrie became famously famous, he took an idea for an operetta to Richard D'Oyly Carte. The impresario suggested Arthur Sullivan as composer but he declined and the job fell to an Ernest Ford. Barrie worked on the libretto of *Jane Annie* only for his creative juices to run dry. In desperation he asked his friend Arthur Conan Doyle for help. Barrie's now famous telegram went as follows. "Come at once if convenient; if not, come anyway."

These two went back a long way. Now, decades later, they met under different circumstances. Sticking to the plan discussed with Wood, Barrie fired up Doyle with all manner of chatter and gossip. He built up the drama till he hit the climax.

'Now, Arthur, you will never believe my latest hair-brained scheme.'

'You're right, I won't,' said Sir Arthur.

'I'm re-forming the Allahakbarries cricket team.'

Sir Arthur roared with laughter. Wood and Barrie's plan showed promise. 'You're mad,' cried Sir Arthur.

'I want you involved, Arthur.'

'Nonsense. I'm far too old and you're shorter than when we last played. Can you even see over the top of the stumps, man?'

Barrie thrived in this jocular conversation. It took Doyle far and away from the misery of Mrs Hudson's manuscript. It would need to be even further away once Wood gave his boss the news about the fake German Professor.

'I want you to captain the side, Arthur.'

'Me? Don't be absurd. Apart from constantly travelling and giving lectures, I couldn't run a slow single even if my life depended on it.'

'No, Arthur, I mean non-playing captain. You pop a blazer over your creams, saunter out for the toss, and then retire to the refreshment tent to regale all and sundry with yarns of your incredible life story.'

That stopped Sir Arthur's mocking. The idea appealed. Well done, Sir James. Outside in the hallway, Jean and Woodie listened and allowed themselves to smile ever so slightly.

The boisterous banter and laughter in the study slowed. 'A jolly good idea, James. What japes we had in those mad cricketing days.' Arthur slipped into his joke-telling, anecdote-remembering role.

'You know I can still remember playing for the MCC at the Crystal Palace in the year ...'

'1900,' said Barrie having heard this tale a hundred times.

'I was bowling to a fellow medical man. I think his name was ...'

'W. G. Grace,' added Barrie playing the straight man in the duo.

'Had the blighter caught behind in what was ...'

They spoke together. 'My only first-class wicket.'

Both men laughed, awash with happiness, but alas their joy peaked. From that moment on, it fell, imperceptibly at first but when it gathered snowball momentum, boy did it crash.

'I have news, James, both good and bad,' said Sir Arthur.

'Please, only the good news, Arthur. We're too old for failure. Tell me of your triumphs.'

Doyle became serious. 'You will not believe these two events.' Barrie worried and outside the study, the two eavesdropping listeners felt sick. 'Some unknown woman, insultingly calling herself Mrs Hudson, has written a dreadful book listing the so-called errors in my Sherlockian stories.'

Barrie sounded indignant, playing along, pretending to have never heard the story before.

'How rude,' he said, 'how petty. People can be so envious.'

'It gets worse. My publisher at *The Strand* believes the manuscript is marvellous, wants to publish and, wait for it, wants *me* to write a foreword praising the text to the heavens. Can you believe that?'

'Ignore it, him, her, them,' said Barrie with a wave of his hand. 'Your reputation as a brilliant storyteller, Arthur, is enshrined in history. No base attempt to besmirch your character will ever succeed. Now, about your good news, do tell.'

Sir Arthur felt better thinking about his historical novels. He spoke softly in a reverential tone. 'James, my historical novels have been discovered by academia.'

'What? How wonderful and not a moment too soon.'

'Some German Professor came to study my notes.'

'He was German? Not British?'

'No prophet is accepted in his own country,' said Sir Arthur hurrying to the best bit. 'My historical novels are to be part of a German university's syllabus. At last, James, I am to join the pantheon of great British novelists. I have admired Sir Walter since childhood. Now I can dream to join him.'

In his heart, Barrie wept but for the sake of his friend he acted as if in one of his plays. 'My dear fellow, I could not be happier for you. When is this to happen?'

Sir Arthur slowed. He lacked the finer details—any details. In fact a nagging doubt stirred in the back corner of his brain. He clung to the academic's visit to boost his happiness quotient. He would ask Woodie for details as soon as Sir James departed.

'This academic year,' he said forcing a smile. Barrie did likewise.

Barrie stood tall, all five feet and a whisker of him. 'I must away, Arthur. Friends are expecting me for tea. Do give that cricketing idea a thought and let me know what happens with your academic recognition.'

They shook hands interrupted by the front door being attacked.

'Not more visitors,' groaned Sir Arthur.

'I'll see myself out old man. Cheerio.' He left with Sir Arthur calling after him.

'And tell whoever's at the door I've run off to Timbuktu.'

A minute later, a worried Woodie hurried to find his boss.

'This time I'm absolutely adamant, Woodie—no visitors.'

'I don't think you have a choice, Arthur. It's the police.'

When the age of motoring began in Britain, Arthur Conan Doyle jumped at the chance to be involved. His interest in cars didn't at first match his ability to drive, with one of his less celebrated incidents involving Sir Arthur's vehicle and a farmer's cart filled with turnips.

Taking a blind corner without due care and attention, the farmer and the author got well acquainted—too well. It wasn't so much that Sir Arthur's open-top car filled with turnips, as the fact his diminutive mater sat in the front passenger seat.

"Are you in there, ma'am?"

"Arthur, I'm buried in turnips. Get me out!"

As more cars and better roads kept appearing, the police became better acquainted with road laws and with those who broke them. Sir Arthur did have a few "situations". When Woodie announced the arrival of the police, naturally the author believed the long arm of the law had turned up to discuss the Highway Code, and how Sir Arthur, yet again, managed to re-write it.

The visitor barged in and confronted the homeowner. 'Sir Arthur Colton Doyle?'

'Almost,' said a surprised Sir Arthur. 'And you are?'

'Inspector Lestrade from Scotland Yard.'

'Scotland Yard?' said a surprised and slightly worried Sir Arthur. 'What on Earth are you doing out here in the wilds of Sussex?'

'I demand to see the original copy of the book written by Mrs Hudson.'

Both Woodie in the doorway and Sir Arthur at his desk, groaned as one. Their literary nightmare worsened.

'One moment,' said Sir Arthur. 'Inspector Lestrade is one of the police officers in my stories about Sherlock Holmes.'

'Thank you,' said Lestrade. 'Now we're getting somewhere. Dr Watson stated Mr Holmes solved several cases yet gave me the credit.'

'He did indeed,' said Sir Arthur now playing along with yet another deluded fan of his fiction. 'I can tell you the cases if you're interested.'

'I know the cases by heart and I can tell *you, sir*, the facts are not true,' replied Lestrade. 'But as the cases are now so widely spread, I've given up trying to correct the record.'

'Good for you.' Sir Arthur relaxed, realizing the man belonged to the same misguided group as Mrs Hudson, another of the poor fanatical souls who believe Sherlock Holmes walked this planet as a living human being.

'But I need to know if Mrs Hudson has perpetuated the myth in her book. What's it called, by the way?'

'Do you mean the myth or the book?' Sir Arthur toyed with his visitor.

'I warn you, sir, I am not without influence in the police service and if my good name is impugned in Mrs Hudson's book, legal action may very well follow.'

'Legal action!' snorted Sir Arthur. 'Inspector Lestrade is a fictional character in a series of stories I alone created and which are hugely popular around the world. You're a fool, man, whoever you are. Now kindly leave before I call the police.'

Lestrade fought back. 'I *am* the police,' he snapped, producing his warrant card. 'Unless you show me Mrs Hudson's book immediately, I'll be forced to arrest you.'

Sir Arthur, Jean and Wood were in shock. All were thinking they might need the real police to remove the fictional police. Sir Arthur took control. He picked up the original of Mrs Hudson's book and thrust it at Lestrade.

Sir Arthur roared his reply. 'Right then; here's the damn book. Take it, keep it, but get out of my house!'

This surprisingly quick victory for Lestrade threw the Inspector. He expected to have to use all his wiles—not that he had many—to win the day. He whimpered.

'Oh, I see. Well, thank you, sir.'

'This way, Inspector,' said Wood leading the policeman outside. They went into the garden 'You may wish to sit over there and read the book. Knock on the kitchen door when you've finished.'

More humility from Lestrade who couldn't believe his luck; he wasn't used to winning. He sat and read the notes in the margin. Wood returned to his employer dreading their next conversation.

Chapter 27

ERNEST BALFOUR BEHAVED AS A DUTIFUL son and grandson. His Nan, Florrie, resided in hospital and her prognosis caused family hearts to grieve. Ernest took it upon himself to visit his Nan to save his poor widowed mother the task. The long trek from her village in the Home Counties to the heart of London proved arduous—a bus, a train and a good measure of shanks' pony.

Ernest used his lunch hour to make the trip to Paddington. He knew his Nan's floor, ward and bed. He used to bring flowers until he discovered the family of the woman two beds along pinched them for their relative. Florrie's kind nature and waning mental condition saw the flower thieves undisturbed in their crime spree.

'Hello, Nan,' said Ernest as he arrived and bent to kiss her.

'Oh,' said Florrie being woken from her midday nap.

'It's Ern, Nan. How are you today?'

'Oh not so bad.'

'What did you have for lunch?'

'Hey?'

'Lunch, Nan, what did you have?'

'I think we'll be having lunch soon.'

Ernest told his grandmother the news from home which was more mundane than mundane. His uncle, Florrie's son, still endured his chest cold; his sister, Florrie's granddaughter, is expecting her second child, and most interesting of all, the cat caught a mouse.

'It was in the coal shed, Nan. I suppose that's why we called her Sooty.'

'Who?'

'The cat.'

'Whose cat?'

The banter continued at this scintillating pace until Ernest checked his watch, didn't want to be late back for work, kissed his Nan and left.

He set off along the corridor when he heard a nurse speak in a louder than normal voice.

'Mrs Hudson! Can you hear me, Mrs Hudson?'

Ernest knew the name, of course he did; it had dominated his workplace, his life for the last few days. Ernest backtracked. He peered in the ward and could only see the back of the nurse. Tentatively he moved into the ward. Another nurse saw him, didn't recognize him and so enquired.

'Can I help you, young man?'

'Oh, I'm looking for a lady I know, a Mrs Hudson.'

The nurse, whose voice caught Ernest's attention, turned. 'Is this the lady?'

Yes, yes and yes again. Ernest moved respectfully and smiled at the Mrs Hudson he felt he knew so well. She didn't look chipper. A bandage wrapped itself around her head and her face showed some nasty looking bruises. Her left eye was half-closed and a plaster dominated her nose.

'Hello, Mrs Hudson,' said Ernest. 'I'm Ernest from *The Strand Magazine*. Do you remember me?'

'She finds it hard to speak,' said the nurse. 'Come back tomorrow.'

'I'm sorry she's not well. Please give her my best wishes.'

Ernest smiled and retreated. His mind a whirl, he moved as quickly as possible through the hospital and out into the London sunshine. He ran towards Edgeware Road and stuck gold. A number 6 open top bus provided by the London General Omnibus Company happened along. He paid no attention to the people or shops in Oxford and Regent Streets or elsewhere as he passed through Piccadilly Circus and into the Strand. Once off the bus, his legs worked overtime.

He burst into the office where Herbert explained a typing error to his secretary. Before the boss could demand an explanation, Ernest delivered his news.

'It's Mrs Hudson, Mr Greenhough Smith, she's poorly, sir. She's in St Mary's Hospital with my Nan.'

'Oh no,' despaired the editor although it was difficult to know the cause of his distress—Mrs Hudson's health situation or the fact that the contract he created for the publication of her manuscript still awaited a signature. 'How is she?'

'I wasn't able to find out, but she did appear poorly. Her head is bandaged and her face covered in nasty bruises. She looked frail and the nurse suggested I visit again tomorrow.'

Herbert endured pain. Mrs Hudson's contract sat primed and ready. There were so many people and lines of enquiry active in the search for her, he only needed one little break. It came but dressed as a double-edged sword. Yes, he'd found Mrs Hudson but no, she might never be able to consummate their marriage. No signature meant her manuscript might never see the light of day.

Herbert retired to plan his strategy. One thought crossed his mind concerning her family. If she died, her will would decide everything. Herbert dreaded a beneficiary who would refuse to sign or worse, a contested will being dragged through the courts, or even worse than worse, Mrs Hudson dying intestate.

Who could he ask? Sir Arthur knew nothing of Mrs Hudson so he wouldn't know her family. Inspector Lestrade didn't know Herbert 24 hours after they met. A fleeting thought was the possibility Holmes and Watson might know her family. *No they won't. They don't even know her first name.*

Herbert decided. Doing nothing was not an option. He must take action. He would need a massive slice of luck. He slipped the unsigned contract and copy of her manuscript in his briefcase, told his staff he had business in the City, and set off for St Mary's Hospital.

At the same time, Dame Jean and Major Wood were deep in conversation. They were in the garden at Windlesham keeping an eye on the chap claiming to be a detective from London as he read Mrs Hudson's manuscript. He concentrated and from time to time took out his notebook and scribbled something.

Jean laid it on the line. 'Woodie, the longer you procrastinate, the worse it will be for Arthur.'

'He'll never speak to me again.'

'Nonsense. He admires and respects you, and will thank you for uncovering the fraud preventing him from suffering public ridicule. If he goes public with the Professor's visit, then discovers he was tricked, his misery will be a hundred times worse. It's now or never, Major. It's time for the "into the valley of Death" and all that stiff upper lip business.'

Wood nodded and felt awful. He didn't like delivering bad news at any time, and this was shattering news, made so much harder with Arthur being his dear friend. Jean squeezed Woodie's arm.

'I'll stay here and keep an eye on the weird policeman.'

Wood went off to war. He knocked on Sir Arthur's open door.

'Woodie, if you're here to tell me there are more visitors, I may have to give you your marching orders.'

Wood entered and sat. Sir Arthur sensed danger. 'You may have to give me my marching orders anyway, Arthur, after what I'm about to tell you.'

A silence skipped in and sat in a third chair. 'I don't like the sound of that,' said the writer.

Wood had rehearsed this speech many times. He refined it, kept it short, and made sure it carried both compassion and truth. Now, as the curtain rose, he dried; he forgot his lines. Before he spoke, Sir Arthur beat him to the punch.

'Is this about our friend from Germany?' Wood turned pale and lost his power of speech. 'He's a fraud. But you already know that.'

Wood thought he would collapse. Relief, surprise and then sadness filled his heart and mind.

'Arthur, I'm so sorry. I should have told you sooner. Forgive me.'

'There's nothing to forgive, Woodie. Now, how is that fanatical bumbling Bobby doing with Mrs Hudson's homily?'

Wood ignored the question about Inspector Lestrade. 'I don't understand, Arthur. How did you discover the truth about the academic? And when?'

'There were several clues, old man. One, another crook I knew once popped into the Northumberland Hotel. Two, why would a German academic be interested in my work? Three, and most importantly, why would *any*one be interested? I made some enquiries and heard the news about an hour ago.'

'I still should have told you.'

'Woodie, I've long accepted my writing expertise is best expressed in short stories and detective fiction in particular. I'm not the next Sir Walter Scott and never will be.'

'But you are the absolute best when it comes to Sherlock Holmes. Tell me another fictional detective who is better known or more loved than that blighter from Baker Street?'

Sir Arthur smiled. He had achieved much and was grateful.

'Have you any idea who those two men were?' asked Wood.

'No idea at all,' said Sir Arthur.

'James Barrie produced a wild idea.'

'He has many wild ideas. And his visit with his crazy cricketing idea was only to take my mind off my literary woes. What a sound fellow he is.' They paused. 'Although I have no idea how he knew about my situation.' Sir Arthur stared at Wood and mouthed the words, "Thank you".

Wood tried to smile. 'Sir James is indeed a fine fellow. But I'll say this for you Arthur; you're a long way from losing your marbles.'

'Enough of the flannel, Woodie; tell me about Peter Pan's wild idea.'

Wood did smile. 'I rang him when your visitors were here and described the pair. Sir James immediately said it was Sherlock Holmes in disguise with Dr Watson as his chauffeur.'

Sir Arthur laughed at the notion although his amusement died because a loud banging sound and a raised voice stopped everything. Jean burst in.

'Arthur, that policeman's gone mad. You'll have to call the police.'

'Sir Arthur remained calm. 'Nonsense, I know the fellow, I fathered him. His bark is worse than his bite. Bring him in, Woodie.'

Inspector Lestrade barged in, hot under the collar, demanding satisfaction.

'This new book is outrageous. I've read the whole book plus the handwritten notes in the margins.'

'And?' teased Sir Arthur.

'And not only are Dr Watson's slurs *not* corrected, I'm not even mentioned—not once!'

'I'm so sorry,' said Sir Arthur, a relaxed and happy chappy. 'You would appear to have made a long journey for nothing.'

'I'll be speaking to my solicitor about this.' He waved the manuscript. 'And this is the evidence. My legal people will require this document as proof of my being misrepresented and ignored.'

'Well why don't you keep it,' said Sir Arthur.

Lestrade froze. He couldn't speak for a few seconds. 'Sorry?'

'You heard.'

'Did you say "keep it"?'

'Yes, I'd like you to have it. It's yours.'

Lestrade lost the incentive to fight. 'Are you sure?'

'Of course; it's like the thousands of other self-published pathetic pastiches people scribble.'

'Oh, well, if you insist,' mumbled the unsure Inspector not understanding Sir Arthur's cruel putdown.

'I do. And to thank you for doing me such a favour by removing the material, I may have a word with Dr Watson and encourage him to pen a new Sherlock Holmes tale.'

Lestrade beamed. 'Oh, would you? Do you know Dr Watson?'

'Better than anyone, and I will insist the case shows Inspector Lestrade outwitting the great Mr Sherlock Holmes.'

Lestrade's joy overflowed. 'Oh, how absolutely marvellous.' He paused. 'I'm sorry,' he apologised. 'I've forgotten your name, sir.'

Sir Arthur extended his hand and spoke. 'Arthur Carlton Doyle,' he said as Lestrade grasped it and they bade one another farewell.

That missing twinkle reappeared in Sir Arthur's eye and Woodie felt a massive burden simply fly from his back.

Chapter 28

HERBERT TOOK OFF RUNNING. He caught a cab in The Strand and headed for St Mary's Hospital. He didn't think it disrespectful to ask an elderly bedridden woman to sign a publishing contract from her hospital bed. She had approached him. She wanted her tale told. He simply followed her instructions. In fact it would be wrong for Herbert to *not* do what he planned.

Ernest had given his boss the details of Mrs Hudson's floor, ward and bed position. Herbert entered the hospital and made his way to the right floor. He followed the signs and reached the correct ward.

Rather than enter, Herbert paused outside her ward. He glanced in, to confirm the lady's presence although that proved tricky.

She was lying on her back with her head elevated, enabling Herbert to see her bruised and bandaged face. He recognized wisps of her grey hair. Nobody stood near or beside her bed. The end of visiting hours loomed large and Herbert knew he may have only one chance at a successful signing. *It's now or never*, he thought.

Other thoughts peppered his brain. *Will she know me? Will she die? What will I say to any visitors or medical staff?* His task needed diplomacy and luck. He thought about the unbelievable content in her manuscript, and how so many readers of Sherlock Holmes would be eager to buy Mrs Hudson's book. He thought about money.

He worried so walked to the end of the corridor and pretended to be lost. A nurse asked if she could help. He told her the ward he required. She pointed and this time, Herbert would stand beside Mrs Hudson and ask for her signature. No, obtain her signature.

Watson was back at Baker Street. The injury crisis consumed everyone. Holmes should have retired, left London, or at least be trying to. Mrs Hudson remained in hospital. Her book stood ready for publication. Watson's literary agent had been uncovered as a dubious person trying to change the characters created by Dr Watson. Why, even John Watson's name faced being changed to Ormond Sacker.

Sacker worried about Sheridan. Watson never knew Holmes to act the way he had in the last few days. Breaking and entering and disguising himself to spy on someone were not new activities for Holmes. But at his age and having decided to retire, Holmes behaved in a most un-Holmesian way. Normally criticism was water off a duck's back to the consulting detective, but some of the content in Mrs Hudson's manuscript really got under his skin, and he reacted.

Watson decided to have words with Holmes, to challenge his friend's behaviour and was about to do so when somebody knocked on the door of that famous 221B Baker Street address. Both men immediately thought of Mrs Hudson and how she would not be opening the door. They wondered if she ever would again.

'I'll go,' said Watson who toddled off downstairs.

Over decades Holmes became an expert at many things, including the ability to read the footsteps of people who ascended the stairs to his sitting-room. Now Holmes didn't need his special powers. The excited voice of one Inspector Lestrade flew up the stairs.

'Mr Holmes! Mr Holmes!' He burst into the sitting-room with Watson a good few seconds behind.

'Inspector Lestrade,' said Holmes.

Lestrade waved Mrs Hudson's manuscript. 'I have here, sir, a document which reveals a catalogue of mistakes you and Dr Watson have made over many years. Your errors gentlemen, not mine, yours.'

'Congratulations, Inspector,' said Holmes remaining calm without even a hint of discomfort. 'And what do you plan to do with said document, Inspector?'

'Ah, now there's the rub. Because Dr Watson often portrayed me as the bumbling policeman, falsely being given credit for a case which had been solved by you, sir, people considered me a bit of a simpleton and a second-rate detective.'

Both Holmes and Watson objected.

'Not true, Inspector,' said Watson.

'Never second-rate, Lestrade,' said Holmes. 'In fact I once told Watson you were the best of the professionals.'

'You did, Holmes' said Watson.

Lestrade lost only a tiny amount of his bluster. 'Well, that's as may be, Mr Holmes, but there's no use denying this here manuscript. Your mistakes are exposed, and I am about to be vindicated.'

'You mean Watson got it wrong?' asked a mock-shocked Holmes.

'Of course he got it wrong. But soon the truth will out.'

'Congratulations,' said Holmes with no emotion whatsoever.

'What has happened, Lestrade?' asked Watson.

'I have made a pact with your literary agent, gentlemen.'

'You mean Doyle?' asked Holmes.

'Indeed, Mr Arthur Colin Doyle is to have *The Strand Magazine* publish another of your cases in which I am to solve the case, and in so doing, outwit the great Mr Sherlock Holmes.' Lestrade's happiness matched that of a playful puppy. Holmes enquired.

'You say you made a pact, Inspector. May one know the details?'

'It's simple, gentlemen. I return this manuscript to Mrs Hudson and then await my vindication in a new case.'

'May I see the document?'

Lestrade handed it over. 'You may keep it Mr Holmes as a reminder of all your faults and failings throughout your career. It demonstrates, sir, you are not the greatest detective after all.'

'Very kind of you,' said Holmes.

'Well gentlemen, I'll detain you no more.' He walked to the door but stopped. 'No Mrs Hudson, gentlemen? Gone on holiday, has she? She'll be over the moon when she hears my news. Give her my best.'

He left and Holmes and Watson made eye contact. The manuscript landed on the overcrowded table, still covered with unpacked items, and neither man knew what to say until Watson got moving.

'Holmes, we must try and visit Mrs Hudson. It's the least we can do.'

'The very least,' said Holmes collecting his hat and cane and that manuscript. Not waiting for his friend, the consulting detective was out the door, down the stairs and hailing a cab in Baker Street. One arrived as Watson rushed out in time to join his friend.

They alighted at the hospital and headed for their landlady's ward.

They knew her location thanks to young, now not-so-young Stamford and took to the stairs. Arriving at the correct floor, they walked along the corridor. It was a normal day in a busy big-city hospital. All sorts of sounds and activities happened around them until something unusual happened.

You might expect a barney in or outside a pub or among rival supporters at a football match but not usually in a hospital, and hardly in a female ward where most patients were elderly.

Holmes and Watson stopped dead when an argument erupted between a man and three other adults, two of whom were female. All four were visitors.

The loud and intimidating voices captured Holmes and Watson's attention as well as anyone within earshot. Onlookers moved into the ward with hospital staff pushing past them. The crowd swelled.

The dispute pitted three against one. The trio got stuck in, their words and actions full of vitriol, their hand gestures threatening. A hospital orderly tried to calm the situation and failed. Patients in this women's ward were scared. Those near the combatants were terrified.

The cause of the dispute proved hard to decipher as all three of the trio, middle-aged siblings, spoke at once. Their cries packed a punch and it seemed only a matter of time before punches, pushes or slaps began.

'How dare you.'

'You have no right.'

'I'm calling the police'

The man being attacked stood with his back to Holmes and Watson. He tried explaining his situation. It made no difference. The trio moved in and that's when the man being attacked made a stand.

'Look,' he said waving a document. 'This is her work. She brought it to me and asked me to publish it for her.'

Holmes and Watson exchanged glances. They realised the man under attack was Herbert Greenhough Smith.

Watson recognized him from their only meeting thanks to Watson's literary agent Arthur Conan Doyle. Holmes knew of him of course and had seen photos of the editor. They certainly knew about the document Herbert waved.

A senior doctor, a former rugby front-rower, pushed his way through and demanded an end to the altercation. The anger cooled but simmered. The doctor took control.

'This is a hospital with many elderly, vulnerable patients. Your behavior is a disgrace. Now quietly, tell me what has happened?' The quartet all spoke at once.

'Stop!' snapped the doctor. 'Come over here, all of you.' The quartet moved away from the patients and particularly from Mrs Hudson. The onlookers were ordered to disperse. Not all did with Holmes and Watson remaining within earshot. The doctor pointed at one of the two females visitors. 'You.'

She pointed at Herbert. 'We arrived to visit our mother who is poorly, and discovered this man, who none of us know from Adam, trying to get our mother to sign a document. Look at her. You talk about vulnerable patients.' She pointed at Greenhough Smith. 'He should be arrested.' The other family members agreed.

The doctor turned to Herbert now hunched, morose. 'Is this true?'

He sounded resigned to failure. 'Yes.'

The patient's relatives wanted blood. 'Quiet,' ordered the doctor, and his subjects obeyed. He turned to Herbert. 'Explain yourself.'

'Mrs Hudson came to my office having written a manuscript. She asked me to publish it. When I heard she was unwell and in the hospital, I came to ask if she still wanted to go ahead with her book.'

'This is nonsense,' said the other woman. 'Our mother is illiterate. She can barely write her own name, let alone a book.'

Mrs Hudson's son got involved. 'He doesn't know our mother. He's trying to trick her into buying funeral insurance or change her will. He's a criminal.'

'That's not true,' protested Herbert, although in a soft voice.

'Okay,' said the son. 'What's her name?'

Everyone glared at the editor. 'Mrs Hudson.'

'What's her first name?' snapped the son.

Nearby, Holmes and Watson exchanged glances. They were in the same boat as the editor of *The Strand Magazine*.

'See,' said the son as Herbert floundered. The editor put the manuscript on his briefcase and mounted his case for the defence.

'I have several witnesses who saw Mrs Hudson in my office. She even went to Sussex to show her work to Sir Arthur Conan Doyle.'

That statement got the crowd buzzing. Not so Mrs Hudson's family who scoffed. 'That's ridiculous. Our mother has never been out of London; never,' said the son, supported by his sisters' vocal antics.

Holmes and Watson were fascinated and horrified. The burly medical man took control. He pointed at Herbert and the son.

'You and you, follow me. The rest of you, please go about your business and do so *quietly*.'

Most of the onlookers and staff moved. Holmes led Watson to the corridor where many conversations took place.

Despondent, Watson spoke. 'Holmes, we should have stood up for Mrs Hudson. And who were those people claiming she's illiterate?'

'Her family,' said Holmes.

Confusion reigned for Watson. 'I didn't know she had a family.'

'Nor did I. But let's go and visit *our* Mrs Hudson,' said Holmes who set off with Watson struggling to keep pace.

'What?' he gasped. '*Our* Mrs Hudson?' Holmes kept moving. 'Holmes, wait. Please stop.'

He did, outside the ward Stamford took them to earlier. 'Watson, there are two women by the name of Hudson in this hospital, and our friend, the editor of *The Strand*, interviewed the wrong one.'

They entered the correct ward, and spotted their landlady. She saw them. 'Gentlemen,' she smiled with difficulty as they approached.

'How are you, Mrs Hudson?' asked Holmes. 'You're looking so much better.'

'Thank you, Mr Holmes. I'm still stiff and sore but the doctor is pleased with my progress.' She looked at Watson. 'But Dr Watson, you don't look at all well, sir. Are you poorly?'

'Watson suffered a little shock, Mrs Hudson,' said Holmes.

'Oh,' she enquired. 'It's nothing serious I hope.'

'No, madam,' said Watson recovering, 'it's just a case of mistaken identity.' She perked up. Watson explained. 'We witnessed the editor of *The Strand Magazine* trying to obtain the signature of another patient whose name, by sheer coincidence, is Mrs Hudson.'

The landlady took in a sharp breath. 'Here? In this hospital? Holmes and Watson nodded. 'Is this true?'

'She even has the same first name as you,' added Watson, 'Missus.'

She tensed. 'You mean, gentlemen, there is another woman who has written about your literary blunders? I am not the first?'

Both visitors moved to allay her fears as her eyes became moist.

'No, Mrs Hudson. You are the first,' said Holmes.

'And the best,' added Watson. 'Nobody can describe me as a dithering plodder or a plodding ditherer as well as you, Mrs Hudson.'

A passing nurse saw the teary old lady and moved to her. 'Now, now, enough of that,' she said patting the pillows and making sure the visitors could hear her words. 'Are these gentlemen upsetting you?'

The patient defended her "gentlemen". 'Oh no, Sister, these gentlemen are gentlemen. This is my tenant, Mr Sherlock Holmes.'

The Nurse didn't bat an eyelid. 'Oh and I suppose that's Dr Watson stood beside him.'

Watson smiled. 'How do you do, Sister?'

She moved to the visitors, her back to Mrs Hudson, and spoke quietly but with a touch of venom. 'Listen,' she hissed. 'You're the second Holmes and Watson double act we've had in here today. Same acting agency is it? Double booking perhaps?'

Holmes looked shocked with Watson clueless. 'I have no idea what you're talking about, Sister,' said the detective.

'I told the other two to sling their hook and I'm doing the same to you. I'll be back in five minutes and if you two are still here, your next visit will be as patients in the emergency department downstairs. Understand, *gentlemen?*' She glared at them, then turned and smiled at Mrs Hudson and left. The patient heard nothing.

'Is everything all right, Mr Holmes?' she asked.

'Perfectly, Mrs Hudson,' said Holmes. 'But we do need to chat about your now infamous manuscript.'

Chapter 29

'HELLO, WOODIE,' said Mason. 'It's Alfie, your favourite spy.'

Wood laughed. 'Hello to you, my friend. What news pray tell?'

'Ah, straight to the point, Woodie. You sound like that Scottish novelist you work for, or should that be work with?'

'I'm nervous Alfie. Things have happened here with both good and not-so-good results. But a lot is riding on your report.'

'I see, well, let me give you the short answer.' He paused. 'I'm confused.'

Wood didn't know if he should laugh or cringe. 'Is there a short explanation of the short answer?'

Mason laughed. 'I'll try,' he said. 'You know I once trod the boards in my Rep Theatre days.'

'I do and from all accounts you were a handy thespian.'

'I still know a few actors and when I heard your Mrs Hudson—that's the real one, not the fictitious lady—ended up in hospital, I ...'

'What?' interrupted Wood. 'She's in hospital? Is she okay?'

Mason sighed. 'You're going to have to stop interrupting me, Woodie.'

'Sorry, but one question. How did you know she was in hospital?'

'You're asking a former highly trained and successful counter-intelligence officer working for the British Government how he obtains data?'

'Okay, I'll shut up.'

'So I contacted a couple of acting pals, gave them their roles and off they toddled to St Mary's Hospital to interview the woman who wrote the manuscript.'

'That is brilliant, Alfie.'

'The actor who played Holmes is a West End star and his make-up and costume were superb. We had no trouble casting Watson and so after a short rehearsal, they entered stage right.'

Wood desperately wanted to know how it all ended. 'And?'

'As you know the aim was to discover the real name and address of the woman calling herself Mrs Hudson. Obviously she can't be the fictional Mrs Hudson because the one you met is alive and well; no, alive but not well, and in hospital. And as she's a real person, we used the illustrations of Holmes and Watson in *The Strand* to cast and costume our characters. Being a fan of the characters, she would accept the actors as the real thing.'

'Brilliant,' murmured Wood.

'So, my acting chums told her they needed a sample of her handwriting to help solve a new case they're working on. Could she please write her name and address on this notepad they provided. She trusts her tenants and does as asked.'

Silence on the other end of the phone.

'You still there, Woodie?'

'Yes, and I'm not interrupting because I want your happy ending.'

'Well, she starts writing when some bossy nurse came along and asked who they were. Typical actors, they thought they'd convince the nurse they were Holmes and Watson.'

'And?'

'She described them as "adjectives deleted" actors, and if they didn't leave immediately she'd have Professor Moriarty push them off the ledge and into the Paddington Falls.'

'What happened?'

'They left by the stairs.'

'So what did the real Mrs Hudson write?'

'Not much. All she managed was Mrs H, 221B.'

Wood groaned. 'Brilliant, we're back to square one.'

'Sorry old man. My theory is she's a damn clever actress who's come up with a damn clever idea for a book to cash in on the popularity of Sherlock Holmes.'

'I think you're right.

'So what's happened with Arthur?'

Wood brightened. 'Good news there. He's decided to ignore the whole thing. If *The Strand* publish the manuscript, he says he'll not respond. He even gave away the original manuscript.'

'Gave it away?'

'Yes, some loopy police detective arrived demanding to read the document claiming he'd been misrepresented.'

'In the manuscript?'

'That, and the original stories or both.'

Alf Mason hesitated. When he met Alf Wood in London the other day to discuss this whole scenario, Wood asked him to go along with any crazy statement. *Is this one of those comments?*

'What's the name of the officer?' asked Mason.

'Inspector Lestrade.'

'But isn't there a fictional Inspector Lestrade in the stories?'

'There is but this fellow had a warrant card so must have been real.'

Mason quit; he'd heard enough. *Maybe the woman calling herself Mrs Hudson and the gent calling himself Inspector Lestrade are in this together. But what this is, I have no idea and frankly, I don't care.*

'Well I'm pleased Arthur has put this whole thing behind him,' said Mason. 'And the fake German professor episode is finished?'

'Absolutely and Arthur even investigated the fellow himself and discovered the fraud.'

'Brilliant. So I assume I say nothing about any of this unless he raises the topic.'

'Please Alf, and many thanks for your superb efforts. I'll keep you informed of any developments.'

'Good-o. Take care, Woodie. Goodbye.'

Mason hung up and relief washed over him. *It was weird. If wartime spies are clever, devious and cunning, then people pretending to be fictional characters leave them for dead.*

Watson worried about the nurse who threatened to have them ejected. With friends and former colleagues working in this hospital, he didn't fancy others watching while he was frog marched off the premises. Holmes could not have cared less about the threatening nurse.

'Now madam, about your manuscript,' began Holmes.

'Oh, please don't worry about that, Mr Holmes; or you Dr Watson. There are far more important things to discuss.' Both men blanched. 'You need to move to the country, Mr Holmes, and I need get better.'

Holmes recovered. His plan, whatever it was, took shape. 'I have made a decision, Mrs Hudson.' She so wanted to know his proposal although Watson kept looking around for Nurse Horribilis. 'I shall not be leaving Baker Street until you are fully recovered and back in your much-loved abode.'

Mrs Hudson's heart began to sing. 'Thank you, Mr Holmes. That gives me great comfort.'

'Excellent, then everything is settled,' said Holmes preparing to depart. Watson joined the happy gang.

'I'm afraid not, Mr Holmes,' she said, and the detective froze. Watson resumed nurse guard duty. Holmes stared at his landlady requiring an explanation. 'I have decided not to submit my manuscript to *The Strand Magazine* or to any other publication.'

In a ward in St Mary's Hospital, you could hear a collective sigh of relief from a couple of well-known, middle-aged gents.

'I see,' said Holmes who felt he could fly. However, being a natural and inquisitive chap, he wanted an explanation. Watson was thrilled about the non-publication but nervous about remaining. He tried using eye contact and head nods to get Holmes to flee.

'The nurse, Holmes, the nurse,' he whispered.

Mrs Hudson remained calm and businesslike. 'Mr Holmes,' she said, 'I need to have the manuscript placed somewhere for safe keeping. Could you handle that for me?'

'Of course,' he replied. 'And you do know there are two copies of your work, madam?'

'Oh?' she said not knowing if she ever did know.

'Mr Greenhough Smith made a copy for safekeeping.'

'So he did. Do you know where they are?' she asked.

'Indeed, I have both.' He tapped his coat pocket. 'On my person.'

Mrs Hudson and Watson spoke as one. 'Both?'

Holmes explained. 'Inspector Lestrade gave me your handwritten copy earlier today, and just now, Mr Greenhough Smith found himself in a spot of bother in the nearby mistaken identity ward. With him distracted, I picked up the typewritten copy to keep it safe.'

There were smiles all round until Watson cracked.

'Holmes, enemy aircraft at twenty yards.'

Nurse Horribilis bore down from the clouds. Two Sherlocks in a single sortie would look good on her aircraft hit list.

Holmes moved as he spoke. 'Farewell Mrs Hudson. Fear not for your home or your art.'

She gave a feeble wave as Watson used Holmes as a shield and the two friends escaped the nurse's attack.

Elsewhere in the hospital, Greenhough Smith finally left the clutches of the hospital security officer. Two things killed his relief at being free—his Mrs Hudson was the wrong Mrs Hudson, and his copy of her "priceless" manuscript had been nicked.

Could he report the theft to the hospital? Yes. Would they listen to him? Hardly. Could he return and tackle the "right" Mrs Hudson trying for *her* signature? Not a wise move, especially with Nurse Horribilis on the prowl.

Herbert retired to lick his wounds. Without the manuscript or signature, he set off for *The Strand Magazine*, his tail well between his legs.

As Holmes and Watson strolled through London heading back to Baker Street, both men felt as if they'd come through fire. A few days ago, Mrs Hudson's manuscript rocked both men to the core.

They couldn't believe the number of errors in their published cases or the intimate and unknown anecdotes described in the manuscript. They couldn't believe the enthusiasm shown by the editor of *The Strand* to highlight their mistakes and private conversations. And most of all, they couldn't believe Mrs Hudson's intelligence, expertise and wit.

Whatever happened with "that" manuscript in the future would be decided by Mrs Hudson. But first, all that mattered was her recovery.

'When this is all over, Holmes, what do you think will happen to Mrs Hudson? We will have departed good old Baker Street. Will she advertise for new tenants once we've moved to pastures new?'

'I have a strange notion, Watson. Now we've seen the hidden side of the dear lady, how clever she is, how determined, I believe she'll make the most of her years of knowing us and our work.'

Watson stopped in the street. 'Holmes, no! You think she'll publish her manuscript after all?' He hurried to catch up with his friend who kept walking.

'Perhaps she'll find another way to appreciate our relationship.'

'I don't understand.'

'I envisage the day, Watson, when Mrs Hudson will entertain readers of your cases who come to Baker Street to see where we once lived and worked.'

Watson liked the idea but had doubts. 'Do you really think so?'

'Strange as it may seem, I do.'

Watson slipped into fantasy mode. 'That would be wonderful, Holmes—readers interested in where we used to live.'

They strolled basking in the thought that at some time in the future, people might follow with interest the exploits of Sherlock Holmes and his friend Dr John H Watson—Sheridan and Sacker.

A park in a square loomed into view and Holmes entered with Watson following. They sat on a bench and enjoyed the Spring sunshine peeping through the trees beneath which Wordsworth-like daffodils chatted away about the lack of any lake views.

'Watson,' said a serious Holmes. 'I have an idea.'

'When do you not?'

'If Mrs Hudson does publish her manuscript, there is a way we can avoid embarrassment from the mistakes in your writing.'

Watson gasped. He knew his friend would solve the conundrum; when did he not? Watson wanted a resolution. The thought he'd made errors with many being schoolboy howlers, haunted him.

'I see,' was all he said, longing for details of his friend's idea.

Holmes paused before explaining.

'We could play a game, Watson, a trick for us to enjoy, and which would shift the blame from us.'

'I don't follow, Holmes. But you must know that. I've been telling you I haven't understood your reasoning ever since we met.'

'You are not responsible for the many errors in your writing.'

'I'm not?'

'In the world of publishing, it is the job of the proofreader, the editor and sometimes even the printer to weed out typographical slips, incorrect facts and such things as repetition and relevance. Those people are paid to do that. It is their profession.'

Watson pondered the point. 'I understand, Holmes but surely if we make an announcement saying other people are to blame for our mistakes, we'll only highlight the issue we're trying to avoid.'

'Ah, Watson, indeed you are a conductor of light. So we need a new workman, a kind soul willing to accept the mantle of creator.'

Watson nodded having no idea what Holmes was talking about.

'Let's start a rumour, Watson, a rumour which will spread, and spread so far, millions will come to believe it is true.'

'May I ask the nature of this rumour, Holmes?'

'Your literary agent stole your work and put his name to it.'

Watson gasped in amazement. 'Sir Arthur stole my tales?'

'We saw how he wanted to change our names.'

'Ormond Sacker,' said Watson remembering the secrets they uncovered in Sussex. 'He wanted to call you Sheridan Hope.'

'Once the rumour takes hold, people will accept Doyle as the creator, and if and when Mrs Hudson's manuscript is published and sweeps the world, we'll be the heroic investigators and your literary agent will be blamed for the many errors. He wrote them.'

Watson was jubilant. 'Holmes, that is brilliant.' He froze. 'But will it work? And how can we start the rumour?'

'Readers.'

'Readers? I don't follow.'

'You must have observed, Watson, there are people who follow our adventures with great enthusiasm. The sales of *The Strand Magazine* boom because of us.'

'I remember what happened to those sales when people thought you'd been killed. Some 20,000 cancelled their subscriptions.'

'So what is needed, Watson is a plan to fool some of these fanatical readers by allowing them to think they have discovered the truth behind the writing of our adventures.'

'But will it work?' asked Watson who loved the idea of the plan. 'And where will we find these fanatical readers?'

'America. Americans know how to suspend disbelief. They embrace fictional characters. Dickens sailed into Boston where the quayside thronged with Americans calling, "What happened to Little Nell"?'

'You think they'll take it seriously?'

'They love dressing in their finery, attending dinners, investing one another into invitation-only societies, and adopting nicknames with a literary pedigree. Americans love literature.'

Watson almost skipped. 'So we let them think I'm such a humble fellow I allowed my agent to take the credit for writing your cases.'

'Spot on, Watson. But now, on to Baker Street; the game is afoot.'

They headed home and Watson couldn't stop talking. 'Thank you for calling it *our* plan, Holmes.'

He gave his controlled smile. 'It will save our reputations.'

'We need a name for this plan, Holmes. What shall we call it? How about *Operation Switch Authors?* No, no, how about *Sherlock's Secret?* Yes, that sounds perfect.'

Holmes' brain crackled. 'How about *Playing the Game?*'

Watson came alive. 'Brilliant, Holmes. I'll stick to being good old Dr John H. Watson, your friend and fellow investigator, and we'll allow my reports to be listed as written by Arthur Conman Doyle.'

Holmes actually smiled, the first time in more than a week.

They turned into Baker Street, passed the Victorian Bobby outside the museum at Number 239, and headed for good old 221B.

Notes

Arthur Conan Doyle died in 1930, and soon thereafter the local London authority extended Baker Street by making Little Baker Street and Baker Street one. This meant new street numbers and thus a 221B address was born.

When this "real" 221B Baker Street appeared, it was part of a large building housing a branch of the Abbey National Building Society. So with a real address, the postie now had somewhere to deliver the mail addressed to Mr Sherlock Holmes. He, silly chap, forgot to give a forwarding address, and so the bank copped his correspondence. Because so much mail arrived, a member of staff was employed to reply to fans around the world.

Today, the so-called 221B Baker Street address is not 221B. It's about 239 Baker Street. Some enterprising entrepreneur has been given permission to re-number a building and thus create the Sherlock Museum which includes Mrs Hudson's former flat. Fans from around the world drop in for a gander and a souvenir. There's even a Victorian Bobby outside for selfies. Don't necessarily believe him if he claims to be a descendant of Inspector Lestrade.

There is a statue of Mr Holmes in Baker Street as there are elsewhere around the world. Statues of Sir Arthur are less numerous. Even in the city of Doyle's birth, the statue is of the sleuth and not the scribe.

Probably the time to suspend disbelief is when the proprietors of 221B Baker Street start selling jars of honey produced by the little-known apiarist, S. Holmes of Sussex.

Free Mystery

Get your copy now at www.cenfoxbooks.com

Can a six year-old girl crack a homicide case? Facing two tricky murders, the Victoria Police Homicide Squad detectives are struggling. When the young granddaughter of DCI Robbo Robertson spots a clue, hey presto, the mysteries unravel. Two decades later and that little girl has grown up and joined the Homicide Squad.

There are six books in **The Detective Joanna Best Mysteries**.

Meet her as a child when you download your free murder mystery at www.cenfoxbooks.com

The Detective Joanna Best Mysteries

Jo Best is new to the Homicide Squad at Victoria Police. She's bright, good at solving murders and even better at finding herself in trouble. A few people love her and a few don't. Some criminals she meets play rough. Some of her colleagues play rougher. Jo's homicide cases have dead bodies and nasty villains (naturally), a peppering of puns and a solid serve of slapstick. There's even a sprinkling of unresolved sexual tension. Jo later heads off to Paris in pursuit of justice. If you enjoy police procedurals, crime fiction, female sleuths and murder mysteries, Detective Senior Constable Joanna Best is worth a whirl.
www.cenfoxbooks.com

Meet the Author

I always enjoy hearing from readers with their questions and/or comments. I have a quarterly newsletter (Foxy's Follies) with news about my latest books, plays and musicals. It's free. If you'd like to receive a copy, please send a request by email. I never share the email address of my subscribers.

writer@foxplays.com
cen@cenfoxbooks.com

And if you'd care to post a review of my books on Amazon or Goodreads, I'll be most grateful.

Happy reading

Cenarth Fox
www.cenfoxbooks.com

P.S. My plays (now radio plays as well) *The Real Sherlock Holmes, Nursing Holmes* and *Sherlock Stock and Barrel* can be read online at www.foxplays.com